AUTUMN BRIDE

When Major Lagallan suggests to Miss Caroline Hetton that she should marry his young brother, she can hardly believe her good fortune, and at first sight Vivyan Lagallan seems to be the perfect bridegroom; young, charming and exceedingly handsome. Yet upon closer acquaintance, Caroline is disturbed by his wild restless spirit, and discovers that he has a taste for excitement that eventually endangers not only his life, but hers, too.

Books by Melinda Hammond
in the Linford Romance Library:

SUMMER CHARADE
FORTUNE'S LADY

MELINDA HAMMOND

AUTUMN BRIDE

Complete and Unabridged

LINFORD
Leicester

First published in Great Britain

First Linford Edition
published 1998

British Library CIP Data

Hammond, Melinda
    Autumn bride.—Large print ed.—
Linford romance library
1. Love stories
2. Large type books
I. Title
823.9′14 [F]

ISBN 0–7089–5241–0

Published by
F. A. Thorpe (Publishing) Ltd.
Anstey, Leicestershire
Set by Words & Graphics Ltd.
Anstey, Leicestershire
Printed and bound in Great Britain by
T. J. International Ltd., Padstow, Cornwall

This book is printed on acid-free paper

1

THE chapel at Laurel House was invariably cold, and even though the calendar told her it was the first day of August, the young governess sitting with her charges in one corner of the chapel was thankful she had chosen to wear her old-fashioned stuff gown with its long sleeves. The family employed no resident chaplain, and Mr Seymor read a long and, thought Miss Hetton, very apt passage from the Bible concerning the trials of Job, followed by the customary prayers, during which the children shuffled and squirmed uncomfortably, eager to return to the nursery-wing where breakfast awaited them.

At last their ordeal was over. Mr and Mrs Seymor made their stately way out of the chapel, followed by Miss Hetton. The young lady would have preferred to take breakfast with her charges in the relaxed atmosphere of the nursery, but it was Mrs Seymor's firm belief that a mother should take a keen interest in her offspring's education, and to this end she insisted that the young governess should attend her at breakfast every morning in order that she might be informed of her children's progress and issue any new directives that occurred to her. Having thus performed her duty, the good lady then banished her children from her mind until they were brought down to the drawing-room to enjoy half an hour of their parents' time before retiring to bed.

That particular morning, Miss Hetton discovered that her employer was in a highly critical mood. After routine enquiries into the children's education, she launched her attack.

"Thomas and Sebastion were very restless during prayers today," she began, applying butter to a piece of bread with mathematical precision.

"You do not seem to have them properly under your control."

"I will see to it that they behave better tomorrow, ma'am."

"I do not believe you are severe enough with them, or any of the children. I have more than once heard Matilda address you in a most unseemly way."

"I encourage them to look upon me as a friend as well as a teacher."

Mrs Seymor looked at her in surprise.

"My dear young woman you cannot know what you are saying! A governess can never be a *friend* to her charges. Why, it is a sure way to disaster! You allow them too much freedom, with the result that before long they will pay you no heed at all! I cannot condone it. Mr Seymor, pray tell Miss Hetton that such dangerous ideas must not be practised in this house!"

The master of the house looked up from his newssheet.

"Eh — what's that? Oh, quite, m'dear. Not to be thought of," he said, burying himself once more in his paper.

Realizing that argument would not be tolerated, Miss Hetton wisely remained silent.

"Of course you are very young," conceded Mrs Seymor, "but you have been with us for nearly two years, now, and should be well acquainted with the manner of things here. Another thing, Josephine has developed a perpetual sniff. It must be stopped at once."

"She has been suffering from a cold recently, ma'am, but I shall of course attend to it."

"And you will make it plain to them, Miss Hetton, that I will *not* tolerate giggling during prayers."

Miss Hetton was aware that the stifled laugh had come not from her charges but from the young maids in the servants' benches, but she had no wish to expose them to their mistress's wrath and she let the matter rest.

A footman entered with the morning's mail upon a silver tray, which he held out to his master. Mr Seymor reluctantly abandoned his paper and sorted through the letters.

"What's this?" he held up a letter, his brows raised in surprise. "A letter for you, Miss Hetton."

"Now who in the world can be writing to you?" asked Mrs Seymor heavily. "You received a letter from your mama less than a month ago, did you not? You might as well open it now, my dear. If it is bad news you will want to let us know soon enough."

Miss Hetton would have liked to take her letter to the privacy of her own room, but she recognized a command in the lady's words and silently opened the sheet.

"It is from Miss Clove, at the seminary," she said, frowning over the neat copperplate handwriting. "She wishes me to visit her next week, the eighth. She writes that it is most important."

Mrs Seymor's brows drew together.

"That is a Thursday. When you

joined us it was agreed that you would have every *Tuesday* afternoon to yourself."

"Would it, perhaps, be possible to change — " suggested Miss Hetton hesitantly.

The older lady's hard grey eyes snapped with disapproval.

"It is very inconvenient at such short notice."

"Oh, let us not be too hasty, my dear," put in her husband mildly. "You will recall that your sister has taken up her annual residence in Cheltenham and we are to go there next week to visit her for a few days. There can be not the least inconvenience to *us* and I am sure Miss Hetton can make some suitable arrangement for the children. After all, she will only be going to Bath, which is less than five miles from here."

His wife rose.

"Very well, if *you* see no problem, Mr Seymor, there is nothing more to be said," she declared.

Upon this majestic utterance the lady withdrew. Her husband prepared to follow her, gathering up his paper and letters from the breakfast table.

"You must not mind her too much," he remarked to Miss Hetton, smiling kindly upon her. "The running of this house is a great responsibility and it sometimes makes my dear lady a little short-tempered."

Miss Hetton flushed a little, saying: "I assure you, sir, Mrs Seymor has given me no reason to think ill of her. I am very grateful to both of you for employing me, I am well aware that with no experience, finding a position as governess would not have been easy, had you decided against me."

"You came with the very highest references, Miss Hetton, and you have not let us down. You may be sure my wife and I appreciate the excellent service you have given us." He rose. "I will arrange for the chaise to be at your disposal on Thursday next, my dear."

With a friendly smile he gathered up

his papers and left the room, while the governess remained behind, glad of an opportunity to re-read her letter.

Miss Clove's Academy for Young Ladies had been in existence for almost two decades, and it was generally considered to be the best seminary in Bath. Its owner, an indomitable little woman of deceptively frail appearance, attributed no small part of her success to the personal, almost maternal interest she took in each of her charges, but none of them had won her affection more than the young lady taking tea with her that Thursday in her pleasant sitting-room, overlooking the gardens of Queen Square.

"I do hope you did not object to my arranging matters in such a managing way," remarked Miss Clove, looking anxiously at her guest. "With time so short it seemed the wisest course to ask you to come here today."

"Not in the least, dear ma'am. I can only be grateful to you for your continued interest in me. Yet I confess that it was the urgent tone of your letter that brought me here — I certainly did not understand its content!"

Miss Clove glanced up at the fine ormulu clock on the mantelpiece and folded her hands in her lap.

"We still have a little time," she said, "I will try to explain. Some weeks ago I received a communication from a Major Lagallan. He was trying to contact you and asked if I could give him your direction. Of course I immediately replied that I could not divulge such information to a stranger."

"No indeed," replied Miss Hetton, feeling that some comment was required of her. "It is not to be expected that you should. I wonder that he should write to you at all."

"But that is the least of it!" declared Miss Clove, sitting forward in her chair. "It seemed that no sooner had I sent off my reply than the gentleman called here in person! He told me he had expressed himself very ill in his letter, that his business with you could only be to your advantage and if I would but arrange a meeting I should be doing you a signal service." She adjusted her spectacles, a delicate flush upon her faded cheek.

"He was altogether a most personable gentleman, Caroline, and such charming manners! When he asked for my assistance — in a most respectful way — I knew not how to refuse him!"

Miss Hetton allowed herself a tiny smile.

"Taken in by his winning smile, ma'am?"

"By no means! Though I will not say that his countenance is unattractive," returned the other lady, incurably honest, "yet it was the thought that I might be helping *you* that persuaded me to lend him my aid."

"Thus you wrote to me, requesting that I call upon you today."

"Yes. Major Lagallan informed me that he would be here by eleven o'clock to explain everything to you."

"How very mysterious," replied Miss

Hetton, frowning. "I remember there was a Lagallan family at Sandburrows, but why should this gentleman wish to trace me after all this time? It must be all of ten years since we moved from there."

"It wants but a few minutes to the hour," returned Miss Clove, "You will soon be able to ask him."

Even as the ornately gilded clock struck eleven there were sounds of an arrival: voices could be heard on the stairs, and seconds later a gentleman was ushered into the room by a wooden-faced servant. Caroline silently applauded his punctuality, and she studied the newcomer as he made his bow to his hostess. He was well above average height, and wore his fair, curling hair unpowdered. His dark green coat was sober enough, but fitted so admirably that Miss Hetton guessed it came from no provincial tailor. Nankin knee-breeches encased his shapely legs, and as he turned towards her, Caroline found herself looking into a pair of surprisingly gentle hazel eyes.

Having performed the introduction, Miss Clove moved towards the door.

"If you have no objections, there are some matters requiring my attention," she added, with a meaningful look at Caroline, "I shall be in my office, should you need me."

The major opened the door for the lady, remarking as he closed it behind her:

"A lady of the most excellent understanding! It is very good of her to allow me to speak to you alone."

Caroline did her best to appear composed: she waved towards a chair.

"Will you not be seated, Major, and tell me what it is you want of me?"

He took a seat, and studied her for a long moment before replying.

His look was not admiring, and in all honesty she could not blame him: Caroline knew the picture she presented could not be called an attractive one. She was wearing a plain

12

grey gown, its austerity unrelieved by any touch of decoration and her hair, an unremarkable brown, was brushed smooth and dressed close to her head. He had been told she was a governess, and it was not hard to guess that her appearance was more necessity than choice — mothers of hopeful young families did not look favourably upon pretty young servants. The lady's cool grey eyes met his thoughtful gaze.

"I am not what you expected, Major?"

"On the contrary, Miss Hetton. You are every bit as I expected."

A rueful smile touched her lips. "A typical governess! Since it has always been my intention to appear as such I should be gratified to learn that I have achieved that result. However, I am contrary enough to wish it was not so! But I waste your time, sir. How can I assist you?"

"You are the daughter of Joseph Hetton, late owner of Rhyne House, near the village of Sandburrows?"

"I am."

"Perhaps you recall that my family own the adjoining estate."

"I do remember something of the family — Mama was upon good terms with Mrs Lagallan, and there was a son, I believe, a year or so younger than myself. But I cannot in truth say that I know *you*, Major. Are you a relation of the family?"

"I am the present owner of the Lagallan estate. I was at school from an early age, and from Oxford I went into the army, so my visits to the area were infrequent. The boy you remember is my half-brother, Vivyan."

Miss Hetton shook her head, frowning slightly.

"I was still a child when my father sold Rhyne House. My memories are a little faded."

Major Lagallan rose from his chair and walked over to the fireplace, where an empty grate was hidden by a canvas fire-screen, embroidered by some past student at the Academy.

"The lady you knew as Mrs Lagallan was my father's second wife, my step-mother. Her health declined rapidly after the demise of my father some two years ago, in fact she did not last more than a year without him. His estates passed to me, but my step-mother's jointure was secured to her own offspring — that is, to Vivyan. It was left in trust for him until he is five and twenty, or until his marriage, whichever is the sooner." He turned to look directly at her. "That is why I have sought you out, Miss Hetton. I want to know if you would be prepared to marry my brother."

For an instant Caroline thought she had misheard him.

"Is — is this some kind of jest?" she said at last.

"Not at all. My brother is impatient to have the use of his estates, and for this he needs a suitable wife."

"But surely he is capable of choosing his own bride — unless he has some defect — ?" She watched him closely, but her words did not shake his composure. Instead he smiled slightly.

"My brother, Miss Hetton, could choose from any number of ladies, without a doubt, but the key word here is 'suitable'. When my step-mama drew up her will, she was well aware of Vivyan's unsteady character, and she thought that by making his inheritance subject to these conditions, she could prevent him from throwing away his fortune. She appointed two trustees, myself and her only brother, Jonas Ashby, who has use of the Shropshire property at present, and he is in no hurry to remove himself from his comfortable living, and will oppose every bride that Vivyan puts forward."

Miss Hetton raised her brows a little.

"And what makes you think that I would be more successful than any other young woman?"

"Your name appears in the will. You are incredulous, Miss Hetton?

It is true, nontheless. If you wish for proof, I can arrange for you to see the lady's will."

As he spoke she jumped up and took a hasty turn about the room, her hands twisting together as she went.

"But I cannot credit it! I could have been little more than ten years old when she last saw me!"

"As you have already said, your Mama was on very good terms with Mrs Lagallan, and although your family moved away so long ago, my step-mama retained fond memories of you. She was gravely ill when the will was drawn up, she knew she would not live much longer. She proposed that Vivyan should not take early possession of his inheritance except in the event of his marriage to Miss Caroline Hetton or another such lady, deemed suitable by both trustees."

"Forgive me for saying so," she said, her voice not quite steady, "But one would suspect Mrs Lagallan could not have been in her right senses when she

17

wrote that! To put such trust in a girl she had not seen for years — it is incredible!"

"I understand how you feel, Miss Hetton. It is irregular, I agree, but it is binding, nevertheless."

"Yet it can only be a few more years before your brother reaches five and twenty. Can he not be patient a little longer?"

"Vivyan is not yet twenty, and a very impetuous young man. He is also very spirited. I fear that if he is forced to remain at Lagallan House kicking his heels as my pensioner for the next five years he may seek some — unacceptable — outlet for his energies, in which case I fear he will not *live* to see five and twenty."

Her clear grey eyes met his direct gaze without flinching.

"You offer me a charming bridegroom, Major."

"What I offer you, Miss Hetton, is an opportunity to spend the rest of your life in comfort. For all his wildness, my brother knows what is due to his wife. You would be treated with kindness and respect, and be the mistress of substantial properties in Hertfordshire and Shropshire," he paused, regarding her with a faint smile, "I am not asking you to give me your decision this instant. If you are agreeable, I should like you to come to Lagallan House, let us say for one month. You could get acquainted with my half-brother, and if you should decide that you do not wish to marry him, a word to me will suffice. You shall be escorted back to Bath as soon as you desire it."

Caroline stood by the window, motionless, staring unseeingly through the glass. For a full minute after the major had finished speaking she remained there, but at last she returned to her chair and sank down, folding her hands in her lap.

"I would be very foolish not to consider your offer, sir," she began calmly, "My present situation is an unenviable one: to spend one's life at

19

the beck and call of others, and at the end of it to eke out an existence with whatever one has managed to save — I admit it is a spectre that haunts me."

"Very well, then," he replied briskly, "I am returning to Lagallan House tomorrow morning. I shall call here to collect you at noon. Your luggage can follow on when — "

"One moment sir! I fear you go too fast for me," she interrupted him, a note of *hauteur* creeping into her voice. "However unpleasant my occupation, I have a duty to my present employer. I cannot pack my bags and walk out in an instant!"

He regarded her impatiently.

"Very well. When would you be free to travel?"

Miss Hetton bristled at his autocratic manner. She pretended to consider the matter.

"I believe I shall be able to leave Bath at the end of the month."

She thought he did not look very

pleased at this, but he merely bowed his head.

"As you wish. Perhaps Miss Clove will allow my carriage to collect you from here on the twenty-eighth."

2

THREE weeks had gone by since Miss Hetton's interview with Major Lagallan, and she was now bowling along the Somerset lanes in his handsome travelling carriage on her way to Lagallan House. The road from Bath lay across the Mendip Hills, and lowering clouds enveloped the coach in a drizzling mist as they climbed slowly upwards. Caroline pulled her serviceable travelling cloak around her and snuggled her feet into the thick sheepskin rug on the floor of the carriage. This was luxury indeed, she thought, remembering other journeys she had made upon the common stage. She leaned her head against the soft padded leather and gave a sigh of contentment. The idea of enjoying such comforts for the rest of her life was too tempting: Vivyan

Lagallan would have to be a veritable monster before she would refuse to marry him!

Slowly the carriage descended out of the mist, and she caught a glimpse of the familiar flat lands spread out below, stretching eastward to the sea. Her parents had moved from Rhyne House nearly eleven years ago, but she had not forgotten how strangely flat the country was, with small, isolated hills rising like islands from a calm, green sea. The low cloud prevented her seeing the distant village of Sandburrows, with its distinctive headland, but she felt a tremor of excitement when the coach finally reached the lowland, and pulled up at a hostelry to change horses for the final stage of the journey.

The Lagallan coach was well known at the inn, and the landlord himself came hurrying out to offer refreshment. Impatient to be moving on, Miss Hetton refused, but she did step down to stretch her legs for a while. The coachman was standing nearby, keeping a watchful eye on the ostlers as they changed one team of sweating horses for a fresh one. He touched his forelock when he saw his passenger approaching.

"How much longer will we be, do you think?" she enquired.

"Little more than an hour now, ma'am. The major's horses can set a cracking pace." He glanced up at the heavy grey clouds that blanketed the sky. "We're in for some more rain, too, I shouldn't wonder."

Caroline moved away a little, glancing up at the sky, and at that moment the tapboy came up to the coachman with a mug of ale, saying with a wink, "You'd best 'ave your firing piece 'andy, Master John. A little rain don't stop Mad Jack."

The coachman took a long draught of ale.

"Don't you worry, lad. Young Tom will be sitting up beside me with his eyes peeled all the way!" he said, wiping his lips with the back of his large fist.

"What did he mean — 'Mad Jack'?" enquired Miss Hetton, a slight crease between her brows.

"We've been having a spot of trouble hereabouts with a highwayman, Miss, but it's nothing for you to worry about," he reassured her. "The lad I've got with me sits up beside me with his gun, and he's ready to give the rascal a fine welcome!"

Caroline did not look too happy with this reassurance, but she pulled her cloak tightly about her and made her way back to the coach. It was little after three o'clock, but the leaden skies gave the impression of evening and she imagined that this dull half-light would be of great assistance to any cut-throat waiting to waylay them. Feeling more than a little anxious, she climbed into the carriage to resume her journey. Thankfully, her fears were groundless and they reached the winding lanes that led through the village of Crowsham and on to Sandburrows with nothing worse than heavy rain to bother them. It rattled on the carriage roof like thunder. Caroline stared out at the bleak landscape: they had passed Crowsham now, and as the coach swung round another of the innumerable bends she caught sight of her old home, Rhyne House, set back from the road, and sheltered from the sea winds by a belt of trees to the south and west. Another few minutes and her journey would be over, for she remembered it was but a short distance from Rhyne House to Lagallan House. At last the coach slowed to a walking pace and turned into a narrow drive, coming to a halt close to the porch of the house. Caroline threw her hood up over her head and when the steps were let down she moved quickly from the coach to the open door and on into the hall.

As she untied the strings of her cloak and handed it to a hovering footman, a woman approached her, smiling warmly. She was dressed entirely in black, with a tiny black lace cap fitted over her snow-white hair.

"You must be Miss Hetton," she said in a pleasant, friendly voice. "Such shocking weather for your journey. I have had a small fire kindled in your room, so let me take you there at once and you can change out of your wet clothes, for I can see that your gown has got wet just coming out of the coach and into the house! I am Mrs Hollister," continued the little woman, escorting Caroline to the stairs.

"Have I not seen you before?" ventured Caroline.

"Bless you, my dear, I was here when you used to come visiting with your Mama. The old master was my cousin, and I came to look after him when his first wife died. Then he brought home the second Mrs Lagallan and well, her health was never that good, and she was only too pleased to leave the household tasks to me. I remember *you* very well, and many's the time you came along to my room while your Mama enjoyed a comfortable cose with my late mistress, God rest her."

"Yes, I remember now, you always had a glass of lemonade and a cake for me — I used to feel quite grown up visiting you."

They had reached the landing and Mrs Hollister opened one of the doors leading off it and led her guest into a large, pleasant bedchamber.

"Here we are, Miss Hetton. I have had a bed made up in the adjoining dressing-room for your maid."

"Oh, but I have no maid with me."

Mrs Hollister was taken aback, but she recovered almost immediately.

"Now is that not just like the major, to forget to tell me such a thing! Never mind, young Jenny — one of the housemaids — is a very diligent girl, and I shall send her up to you for the present. If she proves unsuitable only give me the nod and we will soon fix you up with another."

"Thank you, you are very kind."

They moved aside as a footman entered with Caroline's small and rather battered trunk.

"I have ordered dinner for five o'clock, so there is no need to rush. Rest a little if you can." Mrs Hollister followed the servant towards the door, where she stopped and turned back. "We meet in the drawing-room before dining. Turn right at the foot of the stairs, and you will see the drawing room door before you, you may remember it."

"I shall find it," replied Caroline, "when shall I meet Mrs Lagallan?"

Mrs Hollister blinked.

"There is no Mrs Lagallan, Miss Hetton."

"But I thought — that is, the major — "

The housekeeper shook her head and smiled.

"No, this is a bachelor's residence, but pray don't be alarmed, you need not fear any impropriety. The major has already requested that I should look after you."

The kindly twinkle in her eyes drew an answering smile from Caroline. "I fear my visit here will cause you a great deal of inconvenience."

"Oh never think it, my dear! I am only too pleased to have a little female company. I must go now, I will send Jenny up to you immediately to unpack your things."

★ ★ ★

Shortly before the dinner hour Caroline made her way downstairs. The rustling skirts of her best silk gown gave her added confidence and in truth she felt in need of it, for as she entered the drawing-room Major Lagallan broke off from his conversation with Mrs Hollister and turned a disapproving frown upon her. She hesitated, wondering if she had unwittingly committed some solecism, but before she could speak the frown had disappeared and was replaced with a friendly smile.

"Ah, Miss Hetton," he greeted her, coming forward. His eyes scanned her quickly. "You look different than when

I saw you in Bath."

"I have changed my hairstyle, sir," she offered shyly.

"That's it," he nodded approvingly. "Much better, curls suit you."

"You are putting the young lady to the blush, Master Philip!" Mrs Hollister scolded him mildly, "Come closer to the fire, Miss Hetton. I know we are not yet out of August, but this constant rain makes everything so dreary, does it not? It is very extravagant, but I like to see a cheerful blaze at such a time."

"I must apologize for my brother's absence," put in Major Lagallan as he led her to a chair. "I understand he drove out about noon and has not yet returned. From past experience I think we will not wait dinner for him."

The meal was pleasant enough, the host was solicitous, Mrs Hollister kept up a flow of easy chatter, but Caroline noticed that the major's eyes frequently strayed towards the clock. They had reached the dessert when the slamming of a door arrested the conversation.

Major Lagallan laid down his fork, but Mrs Hollister stretched out her hand.

"If that is Master Vivyan it is best that I go to him," she said, rising from her chair. "What a scold I shall give him, turning up at this late hour!"

Caroline chuckled as the little lady swept out of the room.

"I should not care to be in 'Master Vivyan's' shoes!"

The major grinned. "Mud-spattered boots, more like! He is a scamp, but I pray you won't judge him until you have more properly made his acquaintance."

"You may be assured I will not do so."

Mrs Hollister came back to the dining-table, clucking like a mother hen.

"The wicked boy quite forgot the day!" she explained, "I told him I should not fob you off with any excuses, Miss Hetton. He must make you his apologies, which he will do when he has changed out of his muddy clothes."

32

Miss Hetton pushed aside her plate: now that she was so close to meeting her prospective husband she felt quite nervous. However, she hoped she was too well-bred to allow her feelings to be visible, and tried to put her nervousness to the back of her mind and concentrate upon the ensuing conversation.

Major Lagallan accompanied the ladies to the drawing-room, where the candles had already been lit and the blinds pulled against the gloomy half-light. They had scarcely made themselves comfortable when the door opened to admit Mr Vivyan Lagallan. He paused briefly in the doorway, surveying the company. Caroline had to admit she was not a little surprised by his appearance. He was not so tall as his brother, yet still above the average, and of slight build, but his shoulders were broad enough to fill his dark blue coat without extra padding, and a white quilted waistcoat fitted admirably about his slim figure. His hair, cut fashionably short, barely reached the velvet collar of his coat, and he used no powder to disguise its raven-black colour. Black knee-breeches and white silk stockings completed his attire, and as he stepped forward the candlelight glinted upon the quizzing glass that hung around his neck on a black ribbon.

He made a graceful bow to Mrs Hollister. "There, Holly, I have made myself more presentable, have I not? Pray will you not regard me a little less sternly — I vow I quake before you!"

"For shame on you, Master Vivyan!" came the sharp reply, "Waste not your charm on me — try if you can to make your apologies to Miss Hetton, though if she has any sense at all she will refuse to speak to you, such cavalier treatment as you have paid her!"

Mr Lagallan turned towards Caroline, and as he approached her she saw clearly for the first time his lean, handsome face with its finely chiselled features.

"Alas, what can I say?" he began with a disarming smile, displaying perfectly even, white teeth, "I have the devil of a memory, and clean forgot you were coming today. Forgive me!"

Caroline could not repress an answering smile. "Your honesty does you no disservice, Mr Lagallan."

He bowed low over her hand and saluted her fingers. When he looked up, his dark eyes were alight with laughter.

"Thank you, ma'am," he replied gravely. He glanced across at the major who, having already presented each of the ladies with a glass of ratafia, was now pouring two glasses of brandy.

"Well, Philip, are you still at odds with me?"

Major Lagallan picked up the glasses and handed one to Vivyan.

"I am used to your ways by now, Viv," he said, smiling slightly, "You have been racing your bays, again, I take it. Did you win?"

"No, nothing like that, merely trying their paces on the beach. There's no team to beat them in this area."

"Master Vivyan, you were never down there today, in such weather?" demanded Mrs Hollister, aghast.

"But of course! A little rain does not worry me."

The housekeeper did not reply, although her countenance said plainly enough that she did not approve, and she bustled out of the room upon some unspecified business.

"Let me refill your glass," offered the major.

Vivyan shook his head, and set his empty glass down resolutely.

"Sorry, but I am promised for a private little party at the Viking — I cannot cry off."

His brother looked annoyed. He said heavily, "Surely you will not be going out again tonight."

Vivyan raised his hands in a helpless gesture. "Alas, I have given my word." He turned to Caroline and took her hand. "A poor welcome I have given you, Miss Hetton," he said contritely, "I shall make amends, I promise you."

He kissed her fingers, swept a mocking bow to his brother, and was gone, leaving Caroline and the major to stare after him.

"Well, Miss Hetton, what do you think now of my little brother?"

"Quite frankly, sir, I am quite dazed!"

"I understand he is very popular with your sex."

"I can well believe it, a veritable Adonis, in fact! His dress too is very — grand. It would not disgrace a town beau, I daresay."

He gave a crack of laughter. "Aye, handsome devil, ain't he? Perhaps you can understand a little that with his passion for horses and fashion he needs his own inheritance. He can squander that any way he chooses, with my blessing! But it is my belief that if he had responsibility for his own property he would soon settle down. Do you think you could risk marriage to Vivyan, or do you prefer your present life-style?"

She could not repress a small smile. "My dear sir, marriage to almost anyone is preferable to the life of a governess!"

She thought she read contempt in his eyes, and her own gaze fell, a slight flush tinged her cheek. Before anymore could be said, Mrs Hollister came back into the room, shaking her head.

"I have just seen Master Vivyan on his way out again — such a terrible night, too! I am sure I do not know how his coachman will find his way, it is as black as pitch!"

"Old John knows every inch of the lanes, Holly," the major reassured her, "Be thankful Vivyan has taken the carriage rather than driving himself."

"I can't even think of it!" declared the widow, shutting her eyes in horror. "When he is out alone, or with only his groom, I can never be easy until he is safe home again. It is my constant dread that one day he will be found in a ditch with his neck broken. 'Tis no different if he is riding — he insists upon travelling as though the devil himself were at his heels."

"Perhaps he is," murmured Major Lagallan.

Mrs Hollister frowned upon him. "Now, Master Philip, I wish you would not talk that way! You know there is no harm in the boy except high spirits!"

"And a temperament spoiled by over-indulgence."

"Well, perhaps Mrs Lagallan *was* a little too lenient with him, but your father was getting older, Master Philip, and with yourself away in the army, who should the old gentleman lavish his affection upon save the boy and his sweet mama?"

"With the result that my dear brother has scant respect for authority and an insatiable love of adventure!" he replied somewhat tartly.

Mrs Hollister noticed then that Miss Hetton was looking a little anxious, and immediately turned her attention to her guest.

"We are neglecting Miss Hetton,

Master Philip. How can we best entertain you, my dear? Shall we have a game of backgammon, or cards perhaps — or shall we just sit and talk?"

Miss Hetton rose, saying, "If you do not object, I should like to retire. It has been a long day and I am a little tired, I am sorry to be so unsociable — "

"But of course you must go to bed, my child, how remiss of me!" exclaimed the older lady, "You must be exhausted with all your travelling. I will accompany you to your room and make sure you have everything you need."

The major bowed to Caroline as she moved passed him towards the door. "Goodnight, Miss Hetton. I beg you will not refine too much upon my criticism of Vivyan. I am extremely fond of him, you know."

She smiled up at him. "I am sure you are, sir. I shall not allow myself to be swayed by any first impression, I assure you."

3

CAROLINE awoke the next morning to find that the rain had ceased and the day was calm and sunny. She sorted through her meagre selection of clothes, deciding what to wear. She was thankful that she had purchased two new day dresses and an evening gown for her visit. She had not expected to find the prospective bridegroom quite so attractive, and she wished that she had spent a little more on her finery, but she was too level-headed to dwell on this, for she had broken into her scant savings for her new clothes, and to have spent more would have been foolhardy: after all, what little money she had left might be needed to pay her way back to Bath, and to provide food and lodging for her until she could find new employment. But that was a gloomy prospect and not one upon which to dwell on such a glorious day. With sudden decision she put on a new white muslin morning dress trimmed with green ribbon, threaded a gold locket — her only ornament — upon a matching band and tied it around her neck. Then she showed Jenny her new maid just how to brush out her curls, picked up her shawl and set off in search of the breakfast room. She found Mrs Hollister there, enjoying a solitary meal.

"Good morning, my dear. You can have no notion how pleasant it is to have company at breakfast. Master Philip is always up and away at the crack of dawn, and Master Vivyan rarely appears before noon!"

"For brothers they are so very dissimilar," observed Caroline, sitting down at the table.

"As chalk is to cheese!" declared Mrs Hollister. "I swear there was never a more quiet, reserved gentleman than Master Philip, while the other — well, so restless he is, and must always be looking for some new excitement. I'll swear there is no fear in him! You'll forgive me for saying so," she lowered her voice a fraction, although they were alone in the room, "if you can find it in you to take the young master for a husband, it would be just what he needs to settle him down."

"You know the reason for my visit?" asked Caroline, colouring faintly.

"Oh yes! I was present when the will was read out — such a to-do as that was!"

"I expect it was a very melancholy occasion for you," observed Caroline. She was eager to hear more but was too polite to ask directly. Fortunately Mrs Hollister was in a talkative mood.

"Goodness yes. We all felt it, you know, for the mistress was so good and kind, never a cross word to anyone, not in all the years I knew her."

"Were any of the servants present at the reading of the will?"

"Only Stalton the butler and Davies,

Mrs Lagallan's dresser. She left soon after of course. There were bequests to them, you see, and the dear lady left me some of her trinkets, bless her heart. There was a lawyer brought all the way from London for the occasion, too. It seemed such a waste of good money to bring the man all that way just to read a bit of paper, but that is how it was. Then of course there was Mr Ashby, Mrs Lagallan's brother. He was looking very solemn, thinking no doubt that he would soon have to live off his own funds — he had been my mistress's pensioner for years, living at Stanhayes, her Shropshire estate. I do hope I do not appear too disrespectful, Miss Hetton, but that man has such a — a *sly* manner that I cannot like him, and the way he pinches at Master Vivyan it is small wonder the poor boy fires up!" she paused to pour herself another cup of tea.

"Is not Mr Ashby one of Mr Lagallan's trustees?"

"Yes, that is correct, and Master

Philip is the other."

"That cannot be very agreeable for Mr Lagallan," Caroline prompted her hostess gently.

"Heavens, no! I remember we were all gathered in the library, Vivyan was scowling across at Mr Ashby, while Master Philip was sitting quite close to the lawyer from London. When the servants had been told of their settlements they left the room, and the rest of us were all very quiet as the lawyer read the rest of the will, until he reached the part about Master Vivyan not having control of the property until he is five and twenty, or married. Master Vivyan jumps up at that, very annoyed. 'And who is this Miss Hetton?' demands Mr Ashby, very pompous. 'How the d — should I know?' snaps Vivyan. Mr Philip says in his cool way that he thinks you used to be a neighbour, but that you had moved away years ago. Mr Ashby begins to look more cheerful then, and it was obvious to me that he had been thinking that the young master might have been secretly engaged, but now he starts to smile, and rubs his hands together, saying his sister was very wise to place these restraints upon such a hot-headed young fellow. Of course Master Vivyan immediately fires up, and says he will be — well, that he doesn't want his uncle living off his rightful inheritance. That made Mr Ashby smile even more, and say in a very smug tone, 'In that case I suggest you find yourself a suitable wife.' I'm sure it would have come to blows soon after if the major had not ordered his brother out of the room."

"I have noticed that he likes to take command," remarked Miss Hetton dryly, "no doubt it is a military trait."

"It was not quite like that. He merely told Vivyan that if he wished to express himself in such terms he had best do so in the garden, and to remember that there was a lady present — meaning myself of course. That is just like Master Philip, so considerate, and when I think that his Papa had so kindly offered me a home when my own dear Mr Hollister died, and left me without a penny — I really do not deserve such kindness, I have been so fortunate." The good lady dabbed at her eyes, momentarily overcome by this reflection. Then she resolutely blew her nose and continued. "Now, where was I — oh yes. Master Vivyan immediately begged my pardon and set to questioning the lawyer about the clause and if it was binding, but the man seemed to think it was water-tight. It was clear Master Vivyan was not happy about it, and to make matters worse what must his uncle do but remind him that any marriage would need the support of *both* trustees before the conditions were fulfilled. It was a remark calculated to make the boy lose his temper, and he did just that: his eyes positively blazed with anger and he hurled such abuse at his uncle that I was forced to cover my ears. Then he stormed out, never waiting to hear the rest of the will."

"He sounds to me like a spoilt child," put in Caroline frankly.

Mrs Hollister sighed. "I cannot deny it, yet it is not all his own fault, his temper has never known a check. You see, Philip was ten years old and away at school when the old master brought his new bride here, and when she gave him a second son, well, it was wonderful to behold how the old man doted upon him, but he was brought up so differently from Philip. His mama could not bear to part with him, so he did not go away. He had any number of tutors, but he took precious little notice of them, and old Mr Lagallan was in failing health even then and had very little time for anyone. And his mama," she sighed again, "I have said she was a sweet, good-tempered soul, and Master Vivyan would do anything for her, but she refused to believe he was growing into a wild young man until it was too late."

"Poor boy," murmured Caroline.

Mrs Hollister pulled herself out of her reverie and smiled brightly at the young lady.

"Yes indeed 'poor boy', but I am sure it is not such a sad case. Marriage to a good woman can bring him home safe, I am certain."

"Yes, but I am not convinced that I am the *right* woman for him."

The widow smiled confidently at her. "When you know him a little better you will feel differently. He is fatally attractive to every female he meets," she said simply.

Miss Hetton had no time to reply to this, for at that moment the object of their conversation walked into the room. Caroline wondered if he had heard the final comment, but if he had done so he showed no sign of it, merely making his bow to them both before taking a chair beside Miss Hetton. He was dressed for riding in a dark grey morning coat with buckskins and top-boots, but although his attire was simple, the coat was of excellent cut, and the shine upon his boots was almost mirror-like.

"I hope you slept well, Miss Hetton?" he enquired politely.

"Very well, sir, I thank you, but perhaps I should be putting that same question to you — I was informed you never leave your room before noon."

He laughed. "Holly's been telling you about me, has she? I made a supreme effort this morning, Miss Hetton, to rise early, and come in search of you. I thought you might care to come for a drive, to atone somewhat for my shabby behaviour yesterday." He saw her hesitate and added mischievously, "I promise I shall not overturn you."

Caroline chuckled. "You can have no idea how pleased I am to know that! I should very much like to go with you, thank you."

He rose. "Good. I shall have the carriage at the door in half an hour, and bring something warm to wrap around you, there is a fresh wind blowing today."

"Are you not going to eat?" asked Mrs Hollister in surprise.

Mr Lagallan grimaced. "Tea and bread and butter? No, I thank you! I shall ask cook to set me aside a plate of cold meat when I return."

When Caroline had finished her breakfast, it did not take her long to fasten a wide-brimmed straw bonnet over her curls, but she hesitated over the choice of a wrap: she had a very pretty green cape that was an excellent match for her dress, but she knew that it would be much more practical to take the serviceable woollen shawl that had seen her through so many chilly winters as a governess.

"The green is very flattering, Miss," offered Jenny shyly, trying to be helpful, but Caroline had decided.

"There is nothing attractive about shivering to death in an open carriage," she replied, common sense prevailing, and she picked up the woollen shawl and set off down the stairs. Outside Mr Lagallan was waiting to hand her into his carriage, a light-weight curricule, designed for speed.

"Would you like to go to the beach?" he asked her, spreading a rug across her knees, "It will be a little windy, but you are well wrapped."

"Yes, I should like that." She paused, watching as he expertly guided the fresh and lively pair of match-bays through the gateway and into the narrow lane. "I am glad of this opportunity to talk to you," she continued diffidently, "I would like to clarify my situation here, if possible."

"An excellent idea," he agreed. "What do you want to say?"

"That is just it — I do not know how to put it."

"Perhaps you wish to tell me that after our brief meeting yesterday you find that you cannot bring yourself to marry me and you want to return to Bath immediately."

That made her laugh.

"Not quite! When I saw your brother in Bath, he suggested that I come here for a few weeks to see whether — if — "

"To see if you could stomach me for a husband," he supplied helpfully.

"He put it a little more delicately than that, but you have the idea! Only, I do not know what *you* think of the arrangement."

"Oh, I am quite willing to marry anyone to get Jonas Ashby off my estate — now what have I said to send you into convulsions?"

"Your — your brother told me how charming you could be," she said when she could command her voice. "It is *such* a comfort to me to know that my defects are of no account to you."

He grinned at her. "Not very complimentary, was I?"

"You were downright rude!" she retorted.

"Accept my apologies, Miss Hetton! Let me try to explain. My esteemed uncle has been milking Stanhayes ever since I can remember, and the thought of him continuing to live there at my expense makes my blood boil! He is also determined to veto any female I bring forward as a bride, and I have not the least objection to putting forward the one woman he *cannot* reject."

"Well *I* have!" declared Caroline, colouring. "I am willing to consider a marriage of convenience, but to be used as a weapon of revenge — "

"Offends your pride, does it?"

"Of course!"

He brought the team to a stand and swung round to face her, one arm resting negligently along the back of the seat.

"Let me try to put it in more acceptable terms. I want to be my own master. If I have to wait another five years I shall go mad — Philip is very good, and has offered to fund me, but why should *he* have to pay my expenses when I have a perfectly adequate living of my own, if only I were allowed to control it! No, to gain control of my own life I must marry, and it would appear that you are the only woman that my uncle cannot say is unacceptable." He put his fingers under her chin and tilted her face up, forcing her to look at him. "I need you, Caroline. I make you no declaration of love, you are too intelligent to believe I have developed an undying passion for you, but I *can* promise you that if you marry me I will do my best to make you happy. You will be treated with every consideration, allowed a free rein in the running of my houses, and I should not deny you any reasonable request. In exchange all I ask is that you marry me as soon as possible."

Caroline stared up into his dark eyes, unable to break free of their intense gaze. Her heart hammered painfully within her as she realized she was about to make the most momentous decision of her life. After what seemed an age she managed to turn her head away.

"I — I think I accept your offer," she said at last. "I believe I know what is expected of a wife in these circumstances, and I shall endeavour not to fail you. But I should like to consider the matter more fully — before any announcement is made."

He squeezed her hand. "As you wish, my dear. How long do you suggest?"

"Two weeks, perhaps three — "

He set the team in motion. "I do not wish to be unfair to you, Caro, let us say four weeks, that takes us to the end of September. After that we can proceed with all speed. Shall you object if I tell Philip?"

"Not in the least. I think perhaps Mrs Hollister too should be informed how matters stand."

"Very well. We shall introduce you to everyone as a friend of the family, then when we announce our forthcoming marriage we can let them think it was a long-standing arrangement."

"You are assuming neither of us will cry off, Mr Lagallan?"

"But of course — what reason has either of us to do so? And I wish you would call me Vivyan — I shall call you Caroline, with or without your permission — in fact I believe I have already done so!"

"Worse, you addressed me as 'Caro', a familiarity I shall overlook, in the circumstances."

Vivyan laughed. "Very wise of you, my dear!"

They were turning on to the coast road which led through the tiny village of Sandburrows. On one side stood a row of small cottages, some made merely of driftwood collected from the beach, backing on to the sand dunes which were covered with coarse binding grasses and stunted gorse bushes. On the other side stood the church with stone-walled graveyard, and a sturdy parsonage.

"I remember this!" cried Caroline, looking about her with interest, "Mama used to bring me here occasionally, with a basket of food for some poor family, or a parcel of clothes for the vicar to distribute to the needy. There is a crossing to the beach just past the end cottage, is that correct?"

Vivyan nodded. "It may be a little bumpy. I pay some of the locals a few shillings to keep a path through the dunes clear, but it is still heavy going through the soft sand."

Caroline clung on to the seat as they lurched through the winding gap in the sand dunes and down on to the beach. She caught her breath as the fresh breeze, blowing steadily up from the sea, struck her face, tugging at the brim of her hat.

"I had almost forgotten the taste of the sea," she said, her eyes taking in the familiar view.

The water was almost out of sight, but its distant rumble was incessant. A faint, blue-grey mist hid any prospect of the Welsh coast on the far side of the channel, and to the south the flat sands stretched away into the distance. Vivyan turned the curricle northwards where a mile or so ahead of them lay the headland, like some ancient, sleeping monster stretching out into the channel. Caroline took a long deep breath.

"Happy?" asked Vivyan, glancing at her.

"Very I always loved this place!"

Her companion looked surprised. "It has its good points, I grant you, but if you had spent your whole life here, as I have done, you would want to get away, at least for a while."

"Perhaps."

He steadied the horses.

"They are eager to run. If you are not afraid I will give them their heads."

"One moment, please." Caroline untied the ribbons of her bonnet and held it down firmly in her lap. "I am ready now."

He dropped his hands and the bays shot forward, covering ground at an alarming rate. Vivyan glanced at his companion.

"Frightened?"

She laughed, throwing her head back

and enjoying the wind in her face.

"No, I love it!" she cried, exhilarated.

The headland loomed before them, and Caroline thought idly that it seemed so close she could reach out and touch it, yet it was still half a mile away. The soft sand and dunes gave way to pebbles and a sturdy sea wall.

"How do we get off the beach?" she asked as the team's pace slowed.

Vivyan nodded towards the wall. "There's a break in the wall and a ramp further on. Lee, the farmer who rents the land behind the sea defences, brings his cart down here to collect the driftwood."

He turned the carriage towards the opening and they were soon back on the narrow coast road that led back towards Sandburrows. Caroline's face felt warm now that she was sheltered from the constant sea breeze, and the roaring of the water was muted. She put a hand up to her hair.

"I doubt if I shall be able to get the tangles out for at least a week," she said guiltily, putting on her bonnet. "Let us hope this will hide some of the damage."

They returned to Lagallan House on very good terms. Caroline had lost her initial shyness, and felt she need not stand upon ceremony with her companion, so that when they pulled up at the house she told him not to jump down, adding with a smile, "I can easily get myself down from here and you can take your horses directly to the stables."

With these words she alighted nimbly from the curricle and stepped into the house, hoping to make herself a little more presentable before anyone saw her. Alas for good intentions! Major Lagallan was descending the stairs as she reached them. She saw his look of surprise and felt it necessary to explain.

"Vivyan took me for a drive along the beach. The wind has played havoc with my hair — I fear I present a very dishevelled appearance!"

"On the contrary, the sea air has brought a healthy glow to your cheeks and a sparkle to your eyes."

Caroline blushed uncomfortably.

"Oh — I did not mean, that is, I was not looking for a compliment, Major — if I gave you that impression I am sorry for it."

He smiled down at her. "Would you rather I said that you looked as if you had been pulled through a hedge?"

"Yes," laughed Caroline, passing on up the stairs, "at least I know *that* to be the truth!"

4

BY the end of her first week, Caroline had settled comfortably into life at Lagallan House. At Vivyan's insistence, she was upon first name terms with himself and his brother, and she regarded Mrs Hollister in the light of an indulgent aunt. In fact she saw more of this lady than of the other members of the household: Major Lagallan spent most of his day with his agent, or interviewing tenant farmers, and after dinner he would shut himself away in the library working at his accounts. Vivyan's business was more vague, but he went out most evenings, not returning until the early hours of the morning.

Miss Hetton did not object to this lack of attention, for she was quite content to amuse herself and life as a governess had taught her to value any time to herself. She decided to use some of her leisure hours improving her performance upon the pianoforte: Mrs Hollister had informed her that there was a fine instrument in the library, and she assured Caroline there could be no objection to her using it. Miss Hetton was engaged upon her worthy occupation one morning when she heard the library door open and she stopped playing as Major Lagallan entered.

"Pray do not let me disturb you," he said, moving towards his desk. "I have merely come in to collect some papers."

"I did not know you were still here, you are usually gone out by this time . . . "

"I am off to Bristol today."

"Do you — will you be away long?"

"Three nights at the most, I hope. It is the culmination of all the evenings I have spent in this room poring over my ledgers. I am afraid I have been rather a neglectful host. I had hoped Vivyan would look after you, since he tells me you are both agreed upon the match, but that has not been the case."

"No, no, you are mistaken!" she said quickly, "Your brother has been very good — we have been out driving twice, and he has promised to take me riding — "

"You have been gay to dissipation, in fact," he remarked dryly.

"We have had Mr Lagallan's company at dinner most days," she offered defensively.

"If you call three times in a se'ennight 'most days' you are easily satisfied!"

"Major Lagallan, you more than anyone are aware that this match is an arranged affair! You cannot expect your brother to pay court to me as if — as though I were his heart's desire. I believe Vivyan and I understand each other tolerably well."

"I had expected him to provide you with a little more companionship."

He was surprised to see a look of

pain pass like a shadow over her face.

"That is something I have not known since Papa died, six years ago." To break an uneasy silence, she added: "This pianoforte is a delightful instrument. I cannot recall having used a better one."

"It was my step-mother's. I did not know you could play, Miss Hetton."

Caroline smiled, running her fingers along the polished wood that surrounded the ivory keys. "I know enough to teach my younger charges how to play, but I am not at all accomplished. Without music, all I can remember are a few simple folk tunes."

The major sat on the edge of the desk, watching her.

"How long have you been a governess?"

She looked up, surprised at the unexpected question, but she replied evenly, "Since I finished my own schooling. Miss Clove kept me at the seminary to teach the younger girls. When I was nineteen she secured for me a position with a local family."

"And you have been with the same family ever since?"

"Yes. Two years, to date. The prospects were very good: there were seven children, five of them girls and the eldest was only ten, so you see what a secure post I have relinquished to come here!"

He ignored her attempt at humour.

"Why did you not return to your home? You have said that your father died some years ago, but your mother — ?"

The smile died from her eyes. "My mother returned to her family in Devonshire when Papa died. He — he was heavily in debt, you see, and everything had to be sold to pay off his creditors. My maternal relations generously provided funds for me to finish my schooling, but I had no wish to be a further burden to them."

The major swung one booted foot gently to and fro, watching her, as he remarked: "Surely they opposed your decision to seek employment."

She drew a deep breath before replying in an even voice.

"It was made abundantly clear to me from the start that while they were quite willing to look after Mama, they saw not the slightest reason why they should be called upon to support her child." She put up her chin and added defiantly, "I pray you will not feel sorry for me, sir. I am well able to take care of myself, and I abhor pity!"

Before the major could reply, there was the sound of voices outside the door.

"There is no need to announce me, Stalton, I can find my own way," declared a musical, feminine voice, as the door opened to admit its owner.

She was a tall woman, handsomely attired in a russet-coloured riding habit with a matching bonnet fastened over an abundance of rich brown hair. From her position by the pianoforte Miss Hetton could only see the visitor's profile, but that was faultless, with a straight nose, beautifully curving lips, and a delicately sculptured chin. She did not appear to see Caroline, but went immediately towards the major, her hands held out before her.

"Philip, my dear! I do hope you will forgive the intrusion, but I was out riding and made certain you would not object if I just dropped by to see you."

"Of course you are always welcome here, Joanna. Let me present Miss Hetton to you."

Caroline was now able to confirm that the countenance was quite as beautiful as the profile. The eyes were large and dark, and if Caroline thought she detected a cool, considering look in them as they swept over her, it was gone in an instant, and she was treated to a wide, if not particularly warm, smile.

"Caroline, this is Mrs Cley, you may be interested to know that she resides with her brother, who now owns Rhyne House." He turned to

Mrs Cley, adding, "Miss Hetton used to live there, some years ago."

"Really, how fascinating. You must forgive my breaking in upon you like this, but Philip and I are *such* good friends, you see."

Caroline smiled inwardly. Was this beautiful woman warning her off?

"Miss Hetton is an old friend of the family," explained Philip. "We are delighted she has come to visit us."

"Do you intend to make a long stay, Miss Hetton?" inquired Mrs Cley.

"That depends upon circumstances," replied the other lady with a faint smile. "If you will excuse me, I believe Mrs Hollister has an errand for me. Goodbye, Mrs Cley. I look forward to meeting you again."

"Do you have any commission for me while I am in Bristol?" enquired Major Lagallan, holding the door for her.

Caroline shook her head. "No, I thank you. We shall all await your safe return on Thursday, I am sure."

With these words she passed out of the library and made her way to Mrs Hollister's apartments on the first floor, where she found the good lady in her sitting-room. Mrs Hollister looked up and smiled when she saw her visitor.

"Hello, my dear. I was about to pour myself some tea. There is plenty here for two — would you like to join me?"

"Very much, thank you."

Caroline curled up in an armchair and gave a chuckle.

"I feel like a little girl again, sent here out of the way while the grown-ups chatter away in the drawing-room."

Mrs Hollister stirred the tea gently before pouring it into two fine china cups.

"What nonsense. I do trust neither Vivyan nor Philip has had the audacity to 'send you away', as you phrase it."

"Well, I was certainly feeling very much *de trop*. I was in the library with Philip when a Mrs Cley arrived."

"Oh, She's back at Rhyne House, is she?"

"You know her well?"

Mrs Hollister nodded. "She is a young widow who lives with her brother — Mr Ruthwell — at Rhyne House. She has been there for a year or so, and has regularly set her cap at Master Philip."

"I guessed as much from the cold reception she gave me. Will Philip tell her why I am here, do you think?"

"I doubt it. He is very circumspect when it comes to family matters, although he is on very good terms with the lady. She has been away for a few months, but it seems she has come back to plague us."

Caroline looked up in surprise at the unusual acidity in the other's tone.

"You do not care for the lady?" she enquired tentatively.

"Perhaps I judge her too harshly, and Heaven knows what would become of me if she was mistress of Lagallan House, for she would certainly not allow me to continue here as housekeeper. She's one as wants to run everything her own way — but that is not why I do not like her. It seems to me that she is trying to come between Master Philip and his brother. It's Philip she wants, but if Master Vivyan is in the room, she can't help but try to get up a flirtation with him."

"Trying to make Philip jealous, perhaps?"

"If that is so it won't work," replied Mrs Hollister decidedly. "Master Philip is not the sort to stand that kind of nonsense."

"Well, with the major off to Bristol today, we need not worry about that for a few days," replied Caroline comfortably, "and after that, who knows, perhaps the news of Vivyan's forthcoming marriage might put a different complexion upon matters here."

That evening, and the following one, Major Lagallan would have had no call to criticize his brother's behaviour towards his future bride. Vivyan joined the ladies for dinner, and afterwards entertained them most royally with games of chess and backgammon, poetry reading and light conversation. Caroline remembered the major's remarks concerning his brother's charm, and she realized she was being treated to a fine display of it. She did not object, rather she was amused by Mr Lagallan's attentions, and thoroughly enjoyed herself. However, when on the third day he excused himself immediately after dinner and retired to his room complaining of a headache, Miss Hetton suffered no sensation of boredom, but enjoyed instead a comfortable cose with Mrs Hollister before retiring early to bed.

For some unaccountable reason, she found that sleep eluded her. She dozed fitfully, and during one of the many periods of wakefulness she thought she heard the muffled sound of hoofbeats beneath her window. Her chamber was at the back of the house and overlooked the cobbled yard leading to the stables. She listened intently but heard nothing more. The house was silent and she judged it to be well past midnight. She was drifting away into sleep once more when a noise in the room below jolted her wide awake. It was too late for any servant to be about: she tried to listen, but the hammering of her heart filled her ears. It could be the major returned, of course. Her bedroom was directly above the library, and since Philip used the room as his study he would have more reason than most to go there in the middle of the night, but Caroline was not convinced. Perhaps — she went cold at the thought — perhaps it was an intruder. What should she do? She did not like to wake Mrs Hollister or any of the servants in case it was a false alarm. After all, she had heard nothing for what seemed to her a long time. But she could not get back to sleep. Abruptly she sat up and reached for her wrap: she would have to go and investigate if she wished to get any rest that night. She groped for the tinderbox in the table beside her bed, and when she had lighted her candle she grasped the candlestick firmly and tiptoed across to the door. She opened it carefully and paused, listening. Surely she could hear someone moving about below! With pounding heart she went cautiously down the stairs and into the small antechamber that led to the library. She was less than six feet away from the door when it began to open, slowly and silently. Caroline stood rooted to the spot, unable to draw a breath to scream, even when a figure appeared from the darkness of the doorway.

"Good God! Caro! What the devil are you doing here?"

She put a hand to her heart and gave a shuddering sigh of relief.

"Vivyan! Thank goodness it's you!" she whispered hoarsely.

He was carrying his greatcoat over one arm, but as she spoke he threw it down on a chair and came forward to support her.

"Here, let me have the candle before you drop it. You had best come into the library and I'll pour you a brandy. You look devilish queer."

He led her into the room, shutting the door quietly behind them, then sat her down in a chair and went over to the decanter and glasses that habitually stood on a side table.

"Now, you had best tell me why you are wandering all over the house at this ungodly hour," he hissed, carrying two glasses of brandy, one of which he handed to her.

"I thought you were an intruder," she said unsteadily.

"Drink your brandy, my girl — all of it. You're a little fool if you thought that and came down to tackle me all on your own."

Caroline said nothing.

"As a matter of fact I couldn't sleep, and went out for a night ride. I did not bother to tell anyone, because Holly worries so about me. I went farther than intended, and when I got back I found Stalton had bolted the door, so I had to climb in through one of the windows here. The catch is faulty," he explained, "I have often used it."

"Then it had best be fixed," retorted Caroline as the cognac revived her battered spirits, "or the next time I come down there may well be some blood-thirsty villain waiting to cut my throat!"

Vivyan's infectious grin flashed in the candlelight.

"Sorry if I frightened you, Caro! It was very brave of you to come down."

She rose a little unsteadily to her feet.

"Yes, well, I had best get back now, although I doubt if I shall sleep a wink!"

Vivyan took her arm, saying cheerfully, "Of course you will, the brandy will see to that! Come on, I'll escort you upstairs. Do you feel well enough to walk, or shall I carry you?"

"Certainly not, you horrid boy! I am

perfectly able to walk!" She picked up the candlestick and they made their way back to the stairs, pausing only for Vivyan to collect his coat from the ante-chamber.

"You have dropped something." Caroline scooped up a large square of black silk and handed it to Vivyan, who pushed it into one of his coat pockets.

He guided her towards the stairs, one hand under her elbow to support her. At the bottom step he halted.

"Caro, would you be very good and not mention this to anyone? Holly is such a worrier, and if Philip should hear of it, he'll be sure to lecture me for going out and leaving you alone."

"Very well, I will say nothing to anyone."

He caught her round the waist and kissed her soundly.

"That's my girl!" he said warmly. "I am beginning to think we shall deal extremely!"

5

CAROLINE came down to breakfast the next morning looking pale and heavy-eyed. To Mrs Hollister's anxious enquiries she replied truthfully enough that she had passed a disturbed night.

"I expect it was the weather," remarked the older woman comfortably. "I never suffer from it, but I know that many people find it difficult to sleep when there is thunder in the air."

To add emphasis to her words a distant rumble was heard outside, where heavy storm-clouds were gathering ominously.

"I think you are right," agreed Caroline, pouring herself a cup of coffee. "I mentioned it to Jenny, but she seems to have slept soundly all night."

"For myself, I shall rest more

comfortably when Master Philip comes home: I hate to think of him being waited upon by strangers, at some run-down inn, and Heaven alone knows but what the sheets might not be aired!"

Caroline was obliged to laugh.

"I feel sure the major is capable of surviving such treatment for a few nights! Did you worry thus about him when he was in the army?"

Mrs Hollister nodded, "I said a special prayer for him every night," she replied solemnly.

"I believe he saw action against the French?"

"Very little. His papa died soon after the outbreak of war in ninety-three and Philip was needed here to run the estate."

"It must have been very hard for him to leave his men at such a time," remarked Caroline.

"I think it was and yet at that time, two years ago, we all thought that the conflict would soon be over. But it goes on, and now, when we hear of some new defeat in Holland or the Indies I think Master Philip wishes he were free to be with his regiment, but he knows full well he is needed here, and I cannot be sorry to have him with us. The old master's affairs were in a very sorry state, and Master Vivyan was more than the mistress could handle — if you will forgive my saying so, my dear. Master Vivyan is a good boy at heart, but sometimes he lets his temper get the better of him, you see, and then, only Mr Philip can bring him to order."

"You are very fond of them both, are you not?" asked Caroline.

The widow shook off her reverie. "Of course," she replied in her usual matter-of-fact way, "and I shall lose no time in telling Master Philip what a nod-cock he is if he dares to ride home in this weather!"

As she finished speaking another rumble of thunder rolled over the house and the rain began to fall heavily and persistently. The storm continued all day, and as the candles were lit for dinner Mrs Hollister remarked that she did not look to see the major until the morning. However, when dinner was over and she was sitting in the drawing-room contentedly watching Caroline and Vivyan playing at backgammon, there were heard voices in the hall, and a moment later Major Lagallan walked in carrying a large bundle which he set down in a chair.

"Philip, you rogue! What do you mean by coming home at this late hour, and soaked through, to boot?" Vivyan hailed him merrily.

"I could not bear to leave you in charge another day, little brother, for fear of what you might do to my estate," retorted Philip.

His brother laughed and lounged out of the room in search of refreshments for the weary traveller. It was now Mrs Hollister's turn to fuss over the major, and he bore with her very patiently, eventually placing a small package in her hands and bidding her to go away and open it.

"Oh Master Philip if I have told you once I have done so a thousand times not to bring me presents! Oh — " she drew from its packing a small silver brooch. "Seed pearls!" she breathed, "Really, this is too bad of you!"

Master Philip laughed. "I think so too," he replied, "if all I am to get is abuse for my pains!"

He took up the larger parcel from the chair and handed it to Caroline.

"I thought you might like this," he told her quietly.

Without a word she took off the paper to reveal a roll of beautiful green lustring.

"When I saw it, it occurred to me that it would match your eyes — something of a greeny-grey."

Caroline flushed, fingering the material lovingly, moving it to catch its varying sheens in the candlelight.

"Thank you — I am afraid I do not know what else to say."

The major smiled down at her, and for the first time she noticed a similarity between the brothers, that singularly winning smile.

"I remember Mrs Cley telling me of a very tolerable seamstress in Crowsham. I am sure she can make it up for you." He reached inside his coat to produce another, smaller package. "I have also brought you some music. Perhaps the pianoforte can be moved in here and you could then delight us with your playing in the evenings."

She took the music with barely a murmur of thanks, overwhelmed by this unexpected munificence and she was thankful for Vivyan's cheerful re-entry which gave her a chance to regain her composure.

"Here we are!" cried the younger Lagallan, bringing into the drawing-room a tray bearing a bottle and four glasses. "Now we may all drink to the traveller's return."

"Have you dined, Philip?" enquired Mrs Hollister, "If not I can soon arrange with cook for — ”

“Thank you, but I met with Sir Lambert on the road, and stopped to dine with him.”

“Dear Granby,” murmured Vivyan, “our local Upholder of the Peace! And how is the old fool?”

“Not such a fool as you would make him out to be,” responded his brother gravely. “And take care, little brother, for I have invited him to dinner the day after tomorrow and I want you to be here.”

Vivyan bowed. “As you will, Philip. I will be present, *and* I shall be polite to the old fellow, never fear!”

Caroline’s chief concern the next day was to take the lustring to the seamstress in Crowsham and arrange for it to be transformed into an evening gown. Hearing of her errand, Vivyan offered very handsomely to drive her to the village, and they set off together in his curricle, both in high good humour. It was a beautifully warm, sunny day, with only the frequent puddles as evidence of the storm that had raged for the past twenty-four hours.

"Do you know where this dressmaker lives?" asked Vivyan as they bowled along the Crowsham road to the village.

"No. It was Mrs Cley that mentioned it to Philip, I believe."

"Joanna's finery comes from London, I'd swear to it! I'll wager she's only used the woman's services to alter a gown or two."

Caroline's heart sank: what if the seamstress could not make it up in a fashionable mode — she could not bear to think of such a thing.

"Don't look so down, Caro. We can ask the direction at the Viking," remarked Vivyan, observing her gloomy countenance.

Soon the curricle swept into the village of Crowsham. They turned north on to the Bristol road and at the very edge of the village Mr Lagallan brought his team to a stand outside an old whitewashed inn, whose creaking sign swung slightly in the breeze. A serving girl came out of the inn and stood looking up at them, hands on her hips and swaying very slightly. Her bodice was cut low across her ample bosom, and her large, dark eyes were fixed upon Mr Lagallan.

"Mornin' Master Vivyan," she said with a slow, inviting smile curving her generous mouth. "Are you stoppin' 'ere?"

"Sorry Hannah, my dear. Not today. Can you tell me if there's a dressmaker in the village — what's her direction?"

The maid nodded back the way they had come.

"You'll 'ave to go back through the main street. It's Mrs Dempster you'll be wantin'. 'Ers is the little cottage at the far end of the village — green door and lavender outside the window."

With a word of thanks Mr Lagallan turned his team around.

"Will you be comin' this way again

soon?" shouted Hannah as the curricle drew away.

"Not for a couple of days, my sweet!" he cried gaily over his shoulder.

They picked up speed and passed swiftly back through the village, Caroline silently watching the houses go by.

"Jealous?" enquired Vivyan.

"Not in the least," smiled Miss Hetton. "Should I be?"

He reached for her hand and squeezed it. "I am glad you ain't the possessive type — there would be the devil to pay if you took exception to every girl who smiled at me."

"Are there so many?"

"Hundreds!" declared Vivyan, causing Caroline to laugh aloud.

Mrs Dempster's cottage was quickly found and Caroline's worst fears were allayed by the woman's competent manner and willingness to show her the latest work in hand. The material was handed over, together with one of Caroline's older dresses to be used as a pattern guide. Miss Hetton agreed to return the following day, when the seamstress promised to have a selection of sketches put together for Caroline to choose from. Then she was once more sitting beside Vivyan as they made their way back to Lagallan House.

"I am engaged to race these bays against Sam Granby's team at two o'clock — would you like to come and watch?"

"I would love to do so," responded Caroline quickly. "If I could but collect a warmer wrap, first."

"Certainly. We can call in at the house, then I will take you down to the beach and we will wait there for Sammy."

The groom, who was hanging on the straps behind the body of the chaise, growled something inarticulate, making Vivyan laugh.

"Old Bell doesn't like me to race the bays too often," he explained to his passenger.

"It ain't that, Master Vivyan, as well

you know," muttered the groom. "It's the tides."

"Oh don't be such an old worrier," Vivyan told him impatiently. "I'll bring us home safely, never fear."

When they had made their way through Sandburrows village and on to the beach, they found there was no-one else in sight and Vivyan drew his team up on the hard flat sand to await Mr Granby. Caroline looked uneasily at the muddy brown waves, tumbling over each other at the edge of the in-coming tide.

"How long do we have before high tide?" she asked.

"Oh, a couple of hours," replied Vivyan carelessly. "No need to worry about that." He pointed up the beach. "Where we come on to the beach the tide never reaches, except when there is an exceptionally high spring tide, when it might just reach the dunes. You can see further along where the sand dunes form a high bank — that's where you might get cut off. Of course further on towards the headland the high tides are always smashing against the pebbles — that's why old Lee built his sea wall — with Philip's help, of course. It protects his farmland all year round."

They heard a shout and looked around to see two carriages jolting over the soft sand and coming down the beach to join them.

"Hello, Sam. Glad you could make it." He turned to Caroline. "This is Samuel Granby, Caro. His father is Sir Lambert, so no doubt you'll see this reprobate again at dinner tomorrow. Miss Hetton is staying here for a few weeks — family friend."

Mr Granby grinned at this brief explanation and lifted his hat to Miss Hetton.

"'Servant, Miss Hetton. I hope you will not listen to everything Viv says, or he'll have you believing we are all quite as mad as he is!"

"And so are you all!" retorted Vivyan. "The fellow in the second carriage is

Joseph Thirsby. He comes from the other side of Crowsham, but he ain't a bad sort, really."

The introductions over, the three gentlemen set about deciding the course. At last it was agreed that they should make it a straight speed race to the break in the sea wall. Vivyan glanced at Caroline, mischief dancing in his eyes.

"Shall you sit beside me, Caro?"

"Would that not slow you down?" she returned lightly. "The other gentlemen have no such encumbrances."

"With these animals to draw us your added weight would make little difference. I could still beat them by an easy length."

Caroline threw back the rug that was covering her knees and alighted nimbly from the curricle. "No, thank you for your kind offer!" she told him laughing. "I shall seat myself upon yonder log and watch you. *I* have no wish to break my neck!"

Vivyan chuckled at her words and

handed her the rug, saying she might be glad of it. The three grooms were at the heads of their respective teams, and Vivyan suggested that Miss Hetton might like to start the race. She took the proffered white handkerchief and took up her position, holding her fluttering banner aloft. As her hand dropped, the grooms jumped away and with yells of encouragement from their drivers, the teams lunged forwards and thundered off along the beach.

Caroline watched the carriages as they hurtled away, and she was not surprised to see Vivyan's vehicle drawing clear of its rivals. Soon they were too far away for her to see them clearly, and she took her seat on the convenient log to await their return. They came back at the same break-neck speed that they'd gone, with Vivyan leading the field. With barely a check he rushed on towards Caroline. She did not stir as the bays swept down upon her, only at the last minute did Vivyan bring them to a plunging halt scarcely six feet from her. Without a trace of emotion in her countenance, Miss Hetton picked up her rug and handed it to Vivyan, then she took his hand to climb up beside him.

"Horrid boy! Were you trying to cast me into hysterics?" she admonished him, but without heat.

Her companion grinned. "Not I! Merely teasing you, Caro. You have nerves of steel!" he told her admiringly.

"I am beginning to think I shall need them."

"Your pardon, Master Vivyan, but I think we should be going — the tide." Bell's voice interrupted their interchange.

"What's that?" Vivyan looked around at his groom's words and saw the muddied waves creeping ever closer.

"I think you are right, Bell. Come on, let's say goodbye to Sam and Joseph, then we can go home."

A few jovial words of farewell, mixed with promises of dire revenge from Mr Granby, and the carriages were moving towards the dunes. Soon Caroline and her companion were bowling back through the high-banked lanes around Sandburrows and on to Lagallan House. Vivyan checked his team when he spied two riders coming towards them.

"I know that couple," he remarked, slowing to a walk. "Hello, Joanna, Simon." His glance swept over Mrs Cley, a look half amusement, half admiration in his eyes.

"You been rigging yourself out in town again, Joanna?"

She gave him a dazzling smile.

"Yes. Do you like the military cut? It's all the rage now." She ran one elegantly gloved hand over the folds of her velvet skirts.

"It's very flattering," replied Mr Lagallan, his teasing smile much in evidence. "You would present a very fine picture, Joanna, if it wasn't for your mare. Pity she's cat-hammed."

Mr Ruthwell gave a crack of laughter. "I told you that hack wouldn't fool anyone, Jo!" he informed his sister. "Would you believe it, Viv, she allowed herself to be persuaded to buy that showy lump of horseflesh in town, without any reference to me. As soon as I saw those hocks I told her it wouldn't do!"

Vivyan grinned broadly. "Ain't that just like a female, Simon? Never listen to what you say! By the bye, have you met Miss Hetton — she's staying with us for a while."

Mrs Cley gave Caroline a faint, supercilious smile.

"Yes, we have met," she said languidly. "I believe I forgot to mention it to Simon."

Her tone implied that she had not considered the matter worthy of her attention and Caroline, feeling wind-swept and unattractive in her dull brown wrap and an old bonnet, could not in all honesty disagree. However, Mr Ruthwell exchanged a few friendly words with her while Mrs Cley fixed Vivyan with a limpid gaze.

"Is he right, Vivyan? Have I made such a *terrible* mistake buying this horse?"

"Devil a bit, Jo," he returned cheerfully. "We've all been bitten some time or another. If I were you I'd get rid of it as soon as may be and let Simon fix you up with something else. His taste ain't for such a showy piece, but he'll find you a sound animal, never fear."

"Couldn't *you* find me a suitable mount, Vivyan?"

Mr Lagallan shook his head.

"That ain't my line, Jo," he said defensively, "and no matter how long you look at me with those doe eyes of yours I won't change my mind. Your brother will fix you up, or if you don't want his advice ask Philip — mayhap he'll find a horse for you." Vivyan regarded her for a moment, his lips curling into a smile. "If you are wondering if tears might move me, don't. Your tricks won't work on me, my dear," he said softly.

Her eyes flashed, then she laughed, but there was little real humour in it.

"Oh — perhaps I *will* ask Philip." She turned to Mr Ruthwell. "It is time we went on, Simon. You can finish your conversation with Miss Hetton tomorrow at dinner."

"Oh — are you coming over?" enquired Vivyan.

"Yes," affirmed Mr Ruthwell. "We chanced upon your brother earlier today, and he invited us to come to dinner."

"See you tomorrow, then." Mr Lagallan gathered up the reins, casting a last mocking glance at Joanna. "Shall I ask Philip to find you a quiet little ladies' mount, my dear?"

The lady tossed her head. "There is no need to put yourself to that trouble, sir. I shall ask him myself!" she threw at him as they trotted off.

"I fear Mrs Cley was a little displeased with you," ventured Caroline when the riders were out of earshot.

Her companion laughed. "She doesn't

like to think she's been duped."

"Do you mean her horse? I must admit I saw nothing wrong with it."

"Well, it isn't that bad, but Joanna hates to be beaten upon any suit."

"Then it was too bad of you to tease her."

"Lord, Caro, it will do her no harm. Joanna has all the men in the area falling over themselves to please her — including my big brother."

"Are you then immune to her charms?" she asked him, smiling.

"She plays the spoiled beauty too often for my taste. Besides, if Philip has an interest in that quarter it's not for me to queer his pitch."

"Could you do so?"

"Easily." He glanced down at her, his eyes glinting. "Did you not know I am fatally attractive?"

6

AS the guests arrived for dinner
the next day, Caroline found
herself wishing that the green
lustring had been made up and ready
to wear. It was impossible, of course,
since she had only decided upon a style
with the seamstress earlier that day, but
looking at the colourful assembly in the
drawing-room she felt very ordinary in
her grey silk. First came Sir Lambert
Granby and his wife, a very pleasant,
friendly couple and Caroline warmed
to them at once. They had brought
their son, Samuel, whom Caroline had
met at the beach the previous day, and
their daughter Miss Fanny Granby. She
was a very shy young lady of seventeen
years, unused to company and distinctly
nervous. Caroline's experience at Miss
Clove's Academy proved very useful,
and it did not take her long to

put Miss Granby at her ease and find a topic upon which they could converse for half an hour. Mrs Cley and her brother were the last to arrive, appearing just as Mrs Hollister was about to set dinner back thirty minutes, thus saving the housekeeper from the vociferous outrage of Major Lagallan's temperamental cook.

"Joanna always likes to make a grand entrance," murmured Vivyan, moving beside Miss Hetton.

"At least she is sufficiently beautiful to carry it off," replied Caroline softly.

She felt even more insignificant in the presence of Mrs Cley, who had chosen to wear a flowing gown of jonquil crêpe, cut daringly low across her breast, yet she carried herself with such supreme self-confidence that Caroline could not but admire her. Sitting beside Mrs Hollister as the latecomers were shown in, Lady Lambert leaned a little closer to her hostess and murmured:

"That flimsy creation must be all the

rage in town — it will certainly cause a sensation in Crowsham."

★ ★ ★

"Now that," declared Sir Lambert, regarding with satisfaction his now-empty plate, "was just the sort of dinner I enjoy most! A snug little party of friends, no formality, good food and a very decent Burgundy — you are to be congratulated, Philip."

"Thank you," returned the major, raising his glass.

"Aye, you can have no notion how agreeable it is to come here and enjoy m'self for an evening — I've been devilish busy of late."

"You still chasing your highwayman, Sir Lambert?" Vivyan asked him. "I thought you were pretty close to catching 'Mad Jack' by now."

The older gentleman's jovial face took on a more serious look.

"We've searched this area high and low and no sign of the rascally fellow!

He's been sighted, many a time, but we've had no luck catching him."

"Are you talking of the masked robber?" enquired Mr Ruthwell.

Sir Lambert nodded gloomily.

"He struck again Wednesday last — George Bagett's carriage. Took his watch and a couple of guineas. Stopped him at Rook's Bridge just before midnight."

"Hardly seems worth the effort for such small reward," commented the major, sipping thoughtfully at his wine.

"That's the funny part of it," said Sir Lambert. "All he ever gets away with is a trumpery sum — a few gew-gaws, mere trinkets — and sometimes a little money, but never anything substantial. Except once, when he stopped old Lady Forster's coach and took her jewel box, but luckily we managed to pick up his trail on that occasion and tracked him to a barn at Hobbs' Farm — we must have been close that day, because he panicked and went off, leaving the old lady's jewel box in the barn, unopened."

"Your quarry would seem to be a very careless gentleman," observed Vivyan.

"Oh, I have heard he is no gentleman!" put in Mrs Cley eagerly. "I was informed he is a horribly coarse ruffian with no manners at all, is that not so, Sir Lambert?"

"That *is* what I've been told by those that have been robbed," replied the magistrate slowly.

Mrs Cley nodded, her eyes shining as she looked around the table.

"Yes, and he rides up on a great, black stallion, so powerful that no-one can catch up with him."

Major Lagallan looked amused.

"Thus is a legend born," he murmured.

"We shall get him sooner or later, Mrs Cley, have no fear of that!" Sir Lambert declared. "He'll slip up one day, then we shall see him hang!"

"It must be very exciting to encounter a highwayman," mused Mrs Cley.

"After all, it is so dull here, nothing out of the ordinary *ever* happens."

"I doubt you would enjoy the experience of being robbed by a common thief," remarked her brother dryly.

"I should not let him rob me!" she retorted.

Seeing the gentlemen were looking amused, she added haughtily: "He is only a man, after all, and I have yet to hear that he has killed anyone. I certainly should not stand idly by while he took *my* jewels! That would be very milky behaviour — do you not agree with me, Miss Hetton?"

Caroline gave an apologetic smile.

"I am afraid that if there was a pistol pointed at me I should not hesitate to hand over all my valuables."

Mrs Cley was obviously unimpressed by such a prosaic answer and she turned away, hunching one white shoulder.

"What *would* you do, Joanna?" Vivyan asked her.

"Oh I can protect myself, never

fear!" she replied mysteriously.

"Well, for my part I never travel after dark if it can be avoided and I make sure I take with me an extra footman who carries a shotgun," remarked Lady Granby, deciding the subject had been discussed sufficiently. She cast a meaningful glance at Mrs Hollister, who immediately rose and led the ladies away from the table.

"All the talk of highwaymen has made me a little nervous of going home," Miss Granby confided to Caroline as they entered the drawing-room.

"Now for Heaven's sake don't put on any missish airs, Fanny," put in her mama bracingly. "There is nothing to be feared on the short journey to Crowsham, with your Papa and Samuel riding with us as well as the servants. My dearest wish is that the villain will soon be caught, for I am heartily sick of hearing about him wherever I go!"

"How long has he been plaguing you, ma'am?" asked Caroline.

"Oh, these twelve months past, at least. He strikes mostly on the Bridgwater road, but he has been seen just north of Crowsham. He seems to have a fair knowledge of the country, which makes Sir Lambert think he might be local."

"I wish your husband all success in catching him, Lady Granby," put in Mrs Hollister, shuddering. "We should all rest easier in our beds if the villain were locked up."

"For my part I cannot see why you are all making so much fuss," said Mrs Cley languidly, adding, with just a hint of defiance: "No highwayman shall deter *me* from driving into Weston on Friday, even if Simon will not come with me."

"I am sure Mr Ruthwell would not allow you to go alone if he thought you were in any danger," opined Lady Granby placatingly.

Joanna tossed her head, a look of discontent upon her features.

"He is very disobliging," she

complained, "He knows it is only on Friday that he can spare me the carriage for the whole day, yet he says he will not come with me."

"You must know, Joanna, that Friday is the day of the meeting, to decide upon a way of making our roads safer for all of us," explained Lady Granby quietly. "Every gentleman in the area is promised to attend."

"I know it is very selfish of me to object, but I do so want to go to Weston this week, for there are several things I simply must buy — " she broke off with a little tinkling laugh. "But I am being odiously bad-tempered and I mean to say no more about it! Instead I shall tell you all about the fashions in London. I vow I did not realize quite how dowdy I had become until I walked down Bond Street one morning! Of course, everyone is wearing the lightest of muslins now — *à la vestale*, you know. I daresay, Lady Granby, you would be quite shocked to see how scantily clad are some of our fashionable ladies — those of the highest rank, too!"

My lady could scarcely contain a smile as her eyes went once more to the clinging yellow crêpe, but she said nothing, allowing Mrs Cley to talk herself into a good humour.

The conversation continued to range around the latest news from town until the gentlemen came in, and the entrance of a servant with the tea tray brought a further diversion. A chance remark by Sir Lambert reminded Joanna of an earlier discussion.

"Are you going to the meeting on Friday, Philip?" she asked as the major handed her a cup.

"Yes. I have promised to attend."

She pouted, saying: "What a pity — I was going to ask you to escort me to Weston."

"Why don't you ask young Vivyan to go with you," suggested Sir Lambert cheerfully. "He'll not be with us."

Mr Lagallan was standing close to Caroline's chair at that moment, and she heard him mutter angrily: "No — I am not considered old enough to make a useful contribution!"

Mrs Cley's eyes fluttered hopefully to his face.

"*Will* you escort me, Vivyan?"

He shook his head.

"Sorry, Joanna, I have other plans for that day."

Mrs Cley was silent, but she would not let the matter rest there. Her face was thoughtful as she watched Vivyan pull a chair near to Miss Hetton and engage her in conversation.

"Perhaps, Miss Hetton, *you* would care to come with me," she said presently.

Caroline looked surprised.

"Well — I had not thought — that is, I — "

"Oh *do* say you will come," Joanna urged her. "I hate to travel alone."

"I should like to see Weston," Miss Hetton admitted, "and there are several purchases I want to make."

"Good! Then it is settled!" declared

Mrs Cley. "I shall take you up in my carriage." Her eyes travelled once more to Mr Lagallan and catching her look he laughed and shook his head.

"Oh no, Joanna. You won't catch me that way! It makes no difference to me that there are two of you intent upon this journey — I shall not be persuaded to escort you."

"If you will be advised by me, my dear, you will take an extra man upon the box," advised Mr Ruthwell.

Her sister scorned the idea.

"I have no fear of being waylaid," she declared stoutly. "I have already told you that I can defend myself. 'Tis merely that I prefer to have a gentleman in attendance."

"Perhaps it would be wiser to wait until someone is free to escort you," put in Caroline tentatively, but her suggestion was waved aside impatiently.

"No, no, I have set my mind to go within the week, and I will not be put off. Besides, we shall be back long before dark."

"Frightened of our highwayman, Caro?" asked Vivyan, grinning.

Miss Hetton could not prevent an answering gleam in her own eyes.

"Let us say that I would as lief we did not meet him."

Later that evening Miss Granby approached Caroline and asked her if she cared to ride.

"You see," she explained in a shy voice, "Mama and Papa have promised to take me riding upon the headland next Tuesday, and I thought perhaps you might like to come with us."

"I should be glad to — if someone will lend me a horse . . . "

"That's no problem," said Vivyan, "we can find something suitable for you in the stables, can we not Philip?"

"Certainly. There are a couple of mounts there that would suit."

"Perhaps you would like to come along too, Major," suggested Lady Granby, "I know my husband would be glad of a little male company."

The major bowed.

"I should be delighted, ma'am. Thank you."

"What's this — are you planning a ride?" called Mrs Cley eagerly, "Oh, I do so love to ride — "

Lady Granby immediately included her in her invitation and in a very short time it was agreed that they should all go, except Mrs Hollister, who excused herself from the party, pleading her advanced years.

"Shame on you, cousin! What will we do without you to keep us in check?" Mr Lagallan teased her playfully.

"I am much too old to be gallivanting about the country, Master Vivyan," she told him sternly. "I am sure that Sir Lambert is quite capable of dealing with your high spirits, if necessary."

"If you do not go then I think I shall stay at home, too!" declared Vivyan. "My pleasure will be quite destroyed if my favourite lady is not present."

"That is quite enough of your sauce, sir!" retorted Mrs Hollister severely, although his audacious remark had pleased her.

"I think that is a very good idea, Viv," opined Mr Ruthwell gravely. "Without you we shall have an equal number of ladies and gentlemen. A much more comfortable arrangement, do you not agree?"

"And leave you a free hand to cut me out with the ladies — your wits have gone abegging, Simon!" cried Vivyan jokingly. "Don't worry, I shall be there!"

7

TRUE to his word, Mr Lagallan joined the riding party the following Tuesday, but if his intention was to vie with Mr Ruthwell for the attentions of the ladies his strategy was not immediately apparent. He spent the first part of the ride with Mr Samuel Granby, discussing horseflesh, and only when they had reached the springy turf of the headland did he show any interest in female company, when he responded to Mrs Cley's encouraging glances and engaged her in a light-hearted flirtation.

Caroline thoughtfully regarded them as she followed on some distance behind and when Major Lagallan came up alongside her she said, with a smile: "Your brother is in very good spirits today, Major."

His eyes flickered over Vivyan.

"Yes. It surprises me, for I had expected him to be more than a little out of temper, after I told him that his uncle is arriving today."

"I had thought Mr Ashby made regular visits here."

"He used to do so, when Vivyan's mother was alive, but after the stormy scenes at the reading of the will, he has not been near us — perhaps Vivyan has mentioned it to you."

"Mrs Hollister mentioned something about it. But will Mr Ashby think it odd that you are not there to receive him when he arrives — will he not be offended?"

"No fear of that!" he assured her. "As we only received word yesterday that he was coming, he can hardly expect me to rearrange all my plans and Vivyan certainly would not be persuaded to do so! Besides, Jonas invariably dines on the road and it is most likely that we shall be back before he arrives."

Caroline hesitated, then said slowly:

"Could it — do you think Mr Ashby's visit has anything to do with my being here?"

"Very probably. He has several cronies in Bath and would know of my visit there. I have no doubt he was also informed that my coach returned some time later to collect a young lady."

Caroline looked thoughtful.

"Do you think he will try to prevent the marriage?"

"Perhaps. It is certainly to his advantage that Vivyan remains single, but I do not think there is much he can do, unless he unearths some murky secret from your past."

She laughed. "I am afraid my life has been boringly free of scandal! My father lost all his money at the gaming-tables, but that is no uncommon occurrence, I believe."

"Very true."

She looked up quickly, a slight frown in her eyes. His blunt response was unusual and she suspected at first that he was being censorious, but when she looked into his face there was only kindness there, and understanding.

"Are you not going to tell me what a sad wastrel Papa was — or say it was irresponsible of him to die in such a way, leaving his family penniless?" Her tone was light, but the major guessed the effort it cost her to touch on a matter that affected her so nearly.

"It would be a gross impertinence for me to pass judgement upon your father," he said coolly. "You were very fond of him, were you not?"

She nodded, a faint, wistful smile playing at the corners of her mouth.

"Yes, although I did not see him a great deal. Papa spent much of his time in London, leaving Mama to look after me in whatever home we had at the time. Rhyne House was one of our more permanent abodes, we were there for five years before finances dictated that we should sell up. Of course I was at school for much of the year after that and Mama was able to accompany

Papa to town. I think she believed that if she were with him he would not gamble so heavily." She paused, giving a faint, almost inaudible sigh.

"When gaming is in the blood I believe it is almost impossible to curb it," he remarked quietly.

"It was certainly so with Papa. There was a succession of houses, each smaller than the last and in the end he was forced to take Mama to lodgings in town. I never went there — Papa would not countenance it. He struggled to maintain the school fees and insisted that I remain there for the whole year. He used to come to Bath sometimes, to see me, and he would take me out for the day. I was so proud of him then, for he was very tall, and handsome — always dressed in the height of fashion! And I could talk to him about anything, he always listened to what I had to say. No matter how long we had been apart I always felt easy with him. It was my greatest wish that when I left Miss Clove's I should join him and Mama, but when he died — " she stopped, and taking out a small white handkerchief she blew her nose defiantly.

"I am sorry," she continued, blinking rapidly, "I abhor sentimentality."

"So you remained in Bath?"

"Yes. I was fifteen then, and nearing the end of my education. Not that I minded overmuch staying there, for Miss Clove was very good to me."

"You were fortunate in that."

"I think so. Without her help I have no idea what would have become of me, and now — "

"Now, you are about to contract a marriage that will secure you a very comfortable future." He finished the sentence for her.

"'What female heart can gold despise?'" she quoted lightly, then gave a slight, trembling laugh.

"'Tis a melancholy conversation for such a beautiful day, Major! We have fallen quite a way behind the others and must try to catch them up and find some more amusing subject."

"As you wish, but one word of warning, Caroline. Vivyan can never be long in his uncle's company without losing his temper. My brother is a very impetuous young man, don't let him persuade you into any foolish action."

Before she could reply he had urged his horse on and there was nothing for her to do but to canter behind him until they had caught up with the main party.

It did not take them long to travel the full length of the promontory and the party dismounted to rest a little before starting back. They soon split up, leaving their horses in the care of Vivyan's and Sir Lambert's grooms, the only two servants in attendance. Lady Lambert was quite content to find a convenient spot where she could sit upon the soft turf and watch the waves beating gently around the base of the rock, Sir Lambert beside her in silent companionship. Mrs Cley was strolling over the short grass, one hand holding up the train of her riding dress, the other resting lightly upon the major's arm. Mr Ruthwell set off with Miss Granby and her brother to explore one of the rocky beaches on the north side of the headland, and he called to Caroline to join them, but she shook her head, preferring to wander alone with her thoughts. She made her way to the edge of the grass, where springy turf gave way to a tangle of fern and bramble as the ground dropped sharply away towards the water, and she sank down there, gazing out across the channel.

"Do I intrude, Caro? I can easily go away if you so wish . . ."

Mr Lagallan dropped down beside her.

"Of course not," she smiled at him. "I was merely daydreaming."

"And picking violets."

She looked down at the posy of small flowers in her hand.

"Poor things! I should not have culled them: they will die so soon."

Vivyan removed the tiny nosegay from her fingers and tucked it into a buttonhole on his dark riding coat.

"Then first I shall give them a chance to see a little more of the world!" he declared.

He turned to look out across the waters, his eyes narrowed against the steady breeze.

"Lucky flowers," he murmured softly.

"Is that what you would like, Vivyan, to see more of the world?"

"Of course. I have often thought how grand it would be to set sail from here, to travel the world with no ties, no responsibilities."

"Why not?"

He swung around to face her, surprise and amusement in his eyes.

"Do you wish to come with me?"

"No," she said, meeting his gaze squarely. "I was suggesting you go alone — no ties, no responsibilities."

Vivyan laughed.

"Are you serious, Caro?"

"Never more so."

"And what of you, what would you do?"

"Return to Bath. I should not fall into a decline and die of a broken heart, I assure you!" she added, her eyes twinkling.

He took her hand and kissed it.

"You are very sweet, my dear, but I must not be tempted. We can none of us have all that we desire in life. I shall count myself fortunate to have you to wife, and a comfortable income to live upon."

Caroline was silent, but she was not at all convinced that such an ordinary existence would suit this young man. He was so vital, so alive, even now as he sat beside her, looking out to the distant horizon, she was aware of the restless energy pent up within him, the way his glance burned when he was angry, or elated, and as they fixed upon her face, she could even now fancy that she could see tiny demons dancing in his dark eyes.

"I thought I heard Lady Lambert

calling to you, Caroline. You had best go to her," he said, jumping up and holding out his hand to help her to her feet.

"I heard nothing — " she began, but even as she spoke Vivyan was striding off towards the horses, and she was left with nothing to do but to make her way across to Lady Lambert.

That lady was a little puzzled when Caroline asked her if she had called, but she did not labour the point.

"No doubt it was the wind and the gulls," she told Miss Hetton. "Their cries are almost human at times. No matter. Now that you are here come and sit beside me — I should be grateful for your company, for as you can see my gallant escort is exhausted." She waved towards Sir Lambert, who was stretched out upon the grass beside her, snoring gently.

It was close on an hour later when Miss Granby and her two escorts reappeared, the young lady carrying a number of shells that she had collected with the intention of identifying and sketching them. Her mama applauded this worthy object, and suggested that perhaps it was time they resumed their journey. Sir Lambert, roused from his slumbers, declared that he for one was ready for his dinner and he hailed Major Lagallan who came in sight at that moment, Mrs Cley at his side.

"Mighty fine couple they make, eh m'boy?" muttered Sir Lambert, winking at Mr Ruthwell. That gentleman gave the faintest of shrugs.

"Perhaps," he said, "but I doubt Joanna would want to live in the country all year — she would be pining for town as soon as the Season started."

"I'd wager Philip could keep her here content, my boy!" said Sir Lambert slyly.

Simon gave a short laugh, saying: "You'd lose, sir! I know my sister and I've too much regard for Philip to wish for a connection in that direction! It's my belief Joanna would be better paired with some rich lord who would give her the social life she craves."

The party strolled back to where the horses were tethered, Sir Lambert's groom keeping a watchful eye on them.

"Where's Bell — should he not be helping you?" asked the major.

The groom tugged respectfully at his forelock.

"Mr Lagallan's horse was losing a shoe, sir, and Bell has gone back with his master to have it fixed."

"Is anything wrong, Philip?" Mrs Cley enquired when the major brought her mare over to her.

He gave a non-committal answer, and threw her lightly up into the saddle, but as soon as she was settled he went off without a word, leaving the widow to stare after him, somewhat indignant at such cavalier treatment. Once mounted upon his own powerful bay, he caught sight of Miss Hetton, already in the saddle, but at some distance to the rest of the party. He moved towards her and could see that she was trying to adjust her stirrup leather and exposing a very neat ankle as she did so.

Realizing someone was coming up to her, Caroline looked up, blushing a little as she hurriedly shook out her skirts. The major jumped down from his horse and held out the reins to her.

"Hold these for me while I look at your stirrup."

"I assure you it is fine now, sir," said Caroline, blushing still more.

"Don't be silly. You cannot see what you are doing from up there."

Caroline eyed him resentfully.

"I am not one of your raw recruits to be bullied, Major!"

"I am well aware of that, my dear!" he retorted, his eyes glinting as he looked up at her. "Now, shall I lengthen the strap or shorten it?"

"Shorten it, please."

She drew her boot back out of the way, modestly keeping her skirts drawn around her foot.

"There, try that."

"Thank you, sir. That is much better."

He took the reins of his horse from her and remounted.

"Viv's gone," he said, coming up alongside her. "Did he say anything to you?"

"No. Is anything amiss?"

"Probably not. It seems his horse cast a shoe. I suppose he didn't think it worthwhile to tell anyone he was going."

"Is that what you came over to ask me?"

Again she caught a glimmer of that disquieting smile.

"Disappointed, Miss Hetton?"

"Not at all!" she retorted, nettled. "It is what I thought — I should be very conceited to think my charms equal to those of Mrs Cley!"

She spurred her horse on, leaving the major to follow thoughtfully after her.

As soon as she had uttered them, Caroline regretted her words, and a wave of remorse washed over her.

Major Lagallan did not approach her again, and she discovered how quickly a pleasure trip could lose every vestige of enjoyment. At the gates of Lagallan House the party broke up and she accompanied the major along the private road, where she took the opportunity to offer him an apology.

"I should not have spoken as I did," she told him contritely. "It was most improper. My conscience has troubled me for the duration of the homeward journey, believe me!"

"Then consider that your penance, Miss Hetton, and think no more of it. I certainly shall not do so," came the equable reply.

"Thank you," said Caroline quietly.

She felt unusually depressed and very close to tears as they clattered into the stableyard.

"There is one thing I would say," remarked the major as he lifted her down from her horse. "You underestimate yourself, Caroline. Your charms are considerably superior to any other

131

woman of my acquaintance!"

Before she could bring her stunned brain to think of a suitable reply, he had turned and walked away into the stables.

Mrs Hollister had had the foresight to set dinner back to seven o'clock, an exceptionally late hour by her standards, but giving the riders sufficient time to change their muddied garments, but when Miss Hetton presented herself in the drawing-room a few minutes before the hour, she discovered that there was a further delay.

"Master Vivyan came home barely twenty minutes past," explained Mrs Hollister in disapproving accents. "I have told Stalton to wait another ten minutes and after that the young rascal will have to take pot-luck!"

"You are much too soft on the boy, Holly," remarked the major, standing before the fireplace. "If he cannot be punctual he should have his meal sent up to his room, and not inconvenience everyone else."

"Playing the stern autocrat again, big brother?" drawled Vivyan, coming into the room at that point.

"If you wish to call it that," returned his brother coolly.

Vivyan threw out his hands in a gesture of helplessness.

"What could I do? My mare was lame, and Bell's very good but I couldn't bring myself to leave him with her at Crowsham, nor did I wish to ride his scrawny nag home."

"So you whiled away your time as best you could at the Viking," remarked Philip.

A mischievous grin spread across Vivyan's countenance.

"Hannah did her best to entertain me," he murmured wickedly.

Mrs Hollister clucked reprovingly at such an improper remark, but Caroline was not in the least piqued. She caught the major's eyes and turned away, biting her lip to repress the very improper bubble of laughter welling up inside her.

"You should not talk in such a way, Master Vivyan," the housekeeper reproached him. "It is not at all the thing — what in Heaven's name is that commotion?"

The sound of raised voices could be heard outside the drawing-room, then the doors burst open and a stout gentleman hurried in, his grey wig askew and his round, pudding face very red.

"Evening, Jonas, had a bad journey?" enquired Vivyan, eyeing the newcomer with interest.

"Bad?" squeaked the round gentleman, tottering to a chair. "By Gad, sir, I've been brutally attacked!"

8

JONAS ASHBY sank into a chair and mopped his brow. The major handed him a glass of brandy.

"Drink this, and then tell us if you can what happened."

The gentleman took the glass with shaking fingers, but managed to drain it without spilling a drop of its amber contents.

"I've already told you, I was set upon," he replied in a querulous tone.

"Where did the attack take place?"

"A mile or so before the Crowsham turning — where the road passes through a small wood."

"Rooks Bridge?"

"Aye, that's it."

"How many of 'em were there, Jonas?" enquired Vivyan.

"Eh? Oh — I don't know — two or three, perhaps . . . 'twas quite dark amongst the trees."

"Let us have the truth, Ashby, if you please." Major Lagallan's tone was stern, and the older gentleman eyed him resentfully.

"Well, I only saw one — a big, coarse fellow on a black horse, but that don't mean there wasn't more of 'em waiting to pounce! Damn'd coachman didn't even try to put up a fight. One minute we was bowling along quite merrily, and I was thinking what good time we had made, then there's a shout, and the rascally coachman brings us to a halt without the least resistance! And the footman, well! He was worse than useless! Shaking so much I thought he was going to fall off the coach, damn'd idiot!"

Mrs Hollister frowned at Vivyan, whose shoulders were shaking with repressed mirth.

"What happened then?" pursued the major, refilling Mr Ashby's glass.

"I put my head out of the window to see what was amiss, and found myself face to face with the villain."

"You saw his face?" cried Mrs Hollister.

Mr Ashby shook his head impatiently.

"Figure of speech, ma'am! He was wearing a black silk scarf over his face, and a hat jammed down upon his head, and he was all muffled up in a greatcoat, so I couldn't tell you much about the fellow, except he's a damned scoundrel! He ruined my new wig!" Mr Ashby ended, close to tears.

"He did what?" asked the major, startled.

"He trod on it. Snatched it off my head and threw it onto the ground for his horse to trample on! Quesby had to unpack me another from one of my trunks right there in the middle of the highway, before we could continue our journey."

"Did he take anything of value, Mr Ashby?" enquired Mrs Hollister.

"Aye, madam! Ordered me out of the carriage — Quesby too, and made us empty our pockets. He took my watch, snuff-box and my purse — damn his impudence, he had the effrontery to take out a guinea and throw it back to me — for luck! For two pins I'd have knocked him down, if he hadn't been astride that great brute of a horse!"

"My dear uncle, do you mean to tell us that with your coachman, footman and valet in attendance you were unable to put up any resistance — against one man?"

Mr Ashby gave his nephew a look of dislike.

"I would like to know, sir, what *you* would do with a pistol pointed at your head!" he retorted.

Before Vivyan could provoke any further argument, Mrs Hollister rose, saying in a soothing tone: "It must have been a most terrifying ordeal for you, Mr Ashby. 'Tis small wonder if your nerves are disordered. Your room is all ready and I am sure your man Quesby will be waiting for you, so let me show you the way, and then I shall collect one of my powders for you to take — they are most efficacious in situations such as this . . . "

"Well," remarked Vivyan admiringly, when Mr Ashby had been led gently but inexorably away. "You have to hand it to Holly, she knows just how to handle the old fellow!"

"Yes, which is fortunate for us. It is obvious Ashby has been badly shaken and I would have thought you would have more sense than to try to stir up the coals in such a stupid manner."

"Bah! One would imagine the old fool had been near-murdered instead of having lost a few trumperies," retorted Vivyan.

The major regarded him steadily.

"Highway robbery is a serious offence, Viv. Don't write it off too lightly."

The young man met his eyes for a moment, then he jumped up, a scowl darkening his lean, handsome face.

"I know it, Philip! You've no need to preach to me as though I were a child!" he declared before striding out of the room.

Caroline looked up anxiously at the major.

"Can anything be done to stop these robberies?" she asked him.

"I shall ride out tomorrow morning and make a few enquiries, but I doubt if it will prove of much use. The best thing I can do is to take Ashby along to Sir Lambert's meeting on Friday, when I hope we can reach some agreement upon what is to be done. Do you still go to Weston on Friday?"

"Yes — that is, I have agreed to accompany Mrs Cley, although I confess I am a little apprehensive."

"Because of this highwayman? I don't think you have much to fear, but it would be as well to travel home before dusk." He glanced at his watch. "I have no idea how long Holly is likely to be, and I doubt we shall see my brother again tonight, so it behoves us to do justice to my cook's efforts!"

She allowed him to escort her to the dining-room. At first she was a little shy of dining alone with a gentleman, but the major's friendly manner soon put her at her ease, and in a very short while she was engrossed in a lively conversation, as if she had known him for ever. It was not until the covers were removed from the table that Caroline remembered Mrs Hollister, and wondered aloud what had happened to keep her from her dinner.

"I expect Jonas is being especially troublesome," replied the major calmly. "Does it offend your notion of propriety to be alone with me? I am sorry if I have made you feel uncomfortable."

"Not at all, sir! I cannot remember when I have enjoyed a meal more — which surprises me, a little."

"Oh? Why is that?" he asked, leaning back in his chair.

Miss Hetton gave her attention to the delicate task of choosing a sweetmeat from a small silver dish before replying.

"I had the impression that you did not approve me."

"Whatever gave you that idea?" he

demanded, surprised.

She felt her cheeks burning, and dared not raise her eyes to his face.

"Because I have consented to marry Vivyan — merely to secure a comfortable life for myself. I thought you despised me for accepting — "

"Despised you — my dear girl — !"

He reached out his hand across the table, but whatever words he had intended to utter remained unspoken, and his hand dropped to his side as the doors of the room opened.

"So there you are, Caroline! I thought you had retired, when I discovered you were not in the drawing-room. Poor Mr Ashby is in a very sorry state, and fears he has contracted a fever, so I ordered another hot brick to be fetched up to him and by the time I had seen the gentleman comfortably settled in, I knew dinner would be too far advanced for me to join you, so I ordered a tray to be sent up to me."

The housekeeper bustled into the room, the lappets of her snowy white cap dancing behind her as she walked. Caroline rose from her chair.

"I had not noticed the time," she said, almost guiltily. "I will of course come with you to the drawing-room . . ."

"You had best come along too, Master Philip," continued the widow. "Stalton will be bringing in the tea-tray very shortly. Goodness me, sir, why did you not call for more candles, sitting here in this gloom with only one candelabra to light you? Are you trying to make Miss Hetton think you are poverty-stricken?"

The major returned a suitably grave reply to these remarks, but Caroline could not mistake the smile in his eyes as he escorted the ladies to the drawing-room.

Vivyan did not put in a appearance again that evening, nor did Miss Hetton see him until dinner the following day, by which time she had made his uncle's acquaintance. She was engaged in writing a letter to Miss Clove when

Mr Ashby came into the room and introduced himself.

"Afraid I was too shaken up to make my bow to you last night, Miss Hetton," he informed her with an arch smile. "I am sure you will understand, but now we've met I am certain we shall deal famously together."

She drew her hand out of his soft, clammy grasp.

"I hope so, sir," she replied coolly.

"Well now, Miss Hetton," he began, sitting down opposite her. "Tell me how you are liking your stay here. Very out of the way place, eh?"

"I like it very much. Perhaps you are not aware that I used to live close by."

"Quite so, I was forgetting that! And you are to marry my nephew, what?"

Caroline inclined her head, unwilling to commit herself too far. The gentleman looked troubled and shook his head, sighing.

"Dear, oh dear. Not that you are to be thinking I am not fond of the boy — no-one is dearer to my heart, I assure you, but — well, there we are. I have no doubt his wild ways will abate somewhat once the knot is tied."

He saw she was looking confused, and leaned across to pat her hand.

"But mayhap the young rascal's mended his ways already, has he? If so you are to be congratulated, ma'am. I never thought to see it, but after all he's a dog that's young enough to learn new tricks — not yet twenty and as wild as they come! I blame it on m'sister, God rest her — his mama, you know, and an admirable woman in her way, but no authority. I don't believe she ever checked the lad, and as a consequence he was forever falling in and out of scrapes of one sort or another . . . "

Feeling most uncomfortable, and knowing this kind of talk was not without purpose, Caroline gathered up her letter and muttering an inarticulate excuse to Mr Ashby she fled to the tranquillity of her own chamber, where she tried to forget the gentleman's not-so-idle chatter. She managed to finish her letter, by which time Betty arrived to help her dress for dinner. When she had put the final touches to her dress, pinning a small bunch of flowers to her bodice to brighten up the dull bombazine gown, she was ready to make her way downstairs.

Upon entering the drawing-room she was relieved to see the other members of the household already assembled, but as Mrs Hollister began some word of introduction, Mr Ashby forestalled her, coming forward to greet Caroline in the friendliest manner.

"No need to introduce me to this young lady, ma'am. I made bold and presented myself to her earlier today, did I not, Miss Hetton?" He took her hand and led her towards the group, addressing Vivyan as he did so. "Well, you young pup, place a chair for your lady! What a boy he is for forgetting his manners, Miss Hetton," he said indulgently, "I vow you will have your work cut out to teach him how a husband should go on!"

Caroline could think of nothing to say to these unwelcome pleasantries, but Mrs Hollister stepped adroitly into the breach, enquiring after Mr Ashby's health. This proved a fruitful topic, for although he might look very well now, he assured Mrs Hollister that he had spent a very restless night, and only the beneficial effects of the powder she had given him and Quesby's diligent nursing had prevented his being laid up with a fever. Mrs Hollister clucked sympathetically and encouraged him to expound on a detailed account of the ailments that had afflicted him over the past twelve months.

Miss Hetton felt no obligation to attend to this chronicle, and she instead set about coaxing Vivyan out of the sullens. She succeeded very well, reflecting that he was still very much a boy, and although she was but two years ahead of him in age, in temperament the difference was much greater. The truth of her reflections was brought home to her later that evening. Mr Ashby seemed determined to arouse his nephew's explosive temper. Every remark was calculated to rebuke or embarrass the boy, and although she maintained her own composure she could not blame Vivyan when he exclaimed, after some especially wounding remark:

"Are you trying to give Caro a poor impression of me, Jonas? You won't do it, you know — she understands the arrangement too well for that!"

"My dear boy!" exclaimed his uncle, looking hurt, "Whatever gave you that idea? I have nothing but your best interests at heart, I assure you. Frankly my boy, I despair of you at times. You seem unable to take a little harmless quizzing."

Philip, standing behind his brother's chair, laid a warning hand upon his shoulder.

"A universal failing in the young,

I believe," he remarked coolly. There was the faintest trace of *hauteur* in his look, but it had its effect; Mr Ashby was silenced.

After dinner Major Lagallan bore his guest away to play billiards, leaving Vivyan to entertain the ladies, which duty he performed admirably for half an hour, then he announced he was engaged to meet friends in Crowsham. Mrs Hollister was dismayed.

"Must you go?" she asked him. "Your uncle might well be offended to find you set so little store by his visit."

"Not he!" returned Vivyan scornfully. "Jonas knows well enough what I think of him! Besides, I shall be back before midnight. I have promised to meet Thirsby and a couple of others tonight, and I can't let them down."

Vivyan made his bow and was gone, leaving Mrs Hollister to shake her head over him.

"Oh dear," she sighed. "I do hope

he will try to be reasonable, it is so uncomfortable when he is at odds with his uncle — one feels obliged to be civil to Mr Ashby since he is a guest here, but one cannot help noticing that he is constantly pinching at Master Vivyan and it would be better for everyone if he did not come at all."

"Do you know how long he intends to stay?"

"No, but I suspect he has come to see for himself if Vivyan is really planning to marry. Perhaps I misjudge the gentleman, but I fear he may try to make trouble between you and the young master."

"I too have that impression," Caroline agreed. "The sole object of his conversation seems to be to belittle Vivyan and I confess I find it not a little embarrassing."

"I pray you will not let him persuade you against the young man," replied the housekeeper earnestly. "Master Vivyan is very young, but he is in no way a bad-hearted boy."

Miss Hetton shook her head, saying slowly: "I can safely promise you that I shall not allow Mr Ashby to colour my final decision."

9

IT was Friday afternoon, and heavy grey clouds gathering in the western sky brought an early dusk. Mr Ruthwell's carriage bowled along towards Crowsham and the servant sitting up beside the coachman clutched nervously at his shotgun.

"I don't like the look o' that sky," he muttered.

"It won't rain, leastways not before we gets back," said his companion indifferently.

The servant jerked his thumb towards the carriage, saying bitterly: "We'd have been home an hour since and tucking into our dinner by now, if we hadn't had to wait for madam back there to finish 'er shoppin'."

The coachman frowned at him.

"Don't you speak disrespectful of Mrs Cley, Will m'lad. You just remember she's kin to the master."

The servant gave a disparaging sniff but said no more.

They thundered on, leaving the flat, open plains behind them as they approached the Knoll, where the road made its way through the belt of trees at the foot of the hill. They reached the Crowsham turning without mishap, and the coachman was about to congratulate himself upon making good time home when a horseman shot out from the trees just ahead of the coach, causing the leaders to shy badly. With a smothered exclamation the driver brought the team under control and looked up to find the way ahead barred by a great-coated figure upon a black horse. The unknown rider was levelling two pistols at the box in a most menacing way. The coachman wondered why Will didn't blow the rogue's head off, but soon realized that in the confusion the lad had dropped his gun into the footwell, and was even now fumbling to retrieve it.

"Leave it, lad," commanded the stranger in a loud, rough voice. "I could put a bullet through you before you could even take aim."

Will sat up slowly, his eyes popping with fright.

The horseman rode alongside the box, and, still keeping one pistol levelled at its occupants, he reached into the footwell and drew out the shotgun. Never taking his eyes from the box he hurled the weapon into the woods. The coachman braced himself for an explosion, but the much-maligned gun fell to the ground with nothing more than the rustling of undergrowth.

"That's better! Now, me lads, you sit there nice and still while I sees what you're carryin'."

The rider slid from his horse and walked to the carriage door, where Mrs Cley and Caroline were staring out of the window, their faces very white in the failing light. He threw open the door.

"Well well, come on out, ladies, and let's see what you've got for me!"

Despite his cordial tone two pistols waved ominously in their direction and the ladies slowly descended to the road. They stood together, very still, Mrs Cley with her hands tucked inside a frivolous swans-down muff.

"A fine sight for these tired eyes!" he declared jovially, his rough voice blurred by the black scarf wrapped around his face. "As pretty a pair of doves as I've ever seen."

"Coward!" cried Joanna scornfully, "To steal from defenceless women!"

The man gave a deep rumbling laugh, waving one pistol in the direction of the box.

"With those two lusty fellows to protect you? No, lady, you ain't defenceless. But in spite o' that, it ain't my policy to fleece females, especially when they're as handsome as you two — I just demand a little — momento — to remind me of you!" His eyes alighted upon the gold and emerald ear-rings that Mrs Cley was wearing.

"Now there's some gewgaws that would do nicely. Hand over the ear-drops, my pretty!"

"Take them yourself!" retorted the widow, angry spots of colour on her cheeks. "And it would be futile to threaten to shoot me, because I don't believe you would do it!"

"Maybe not, but don't think I wouldn't put a bullet into your manservant," he replied, unmoved. "If you don't want to see bloodshed you'd best do as I say."

Reluctantly Mrs Cley removed her ear-rings.

"That's much more sensible," approved the stranger. He waved a pistol towards Caroline. "And you, little lady. What trinket have you to offer me? I'll take the brooch I can see in your jacket. Bring that and your friend's offering over to me — come on — I won't bite you!"

Slowly Caroline unpinned her brooch,

an inexpensive circle of paste stones set in pinchbeck, and taking Joanna's earrings she walked over to the highwayman. As she approached she looked up into his eyes, the only visible feature between his hat and the silk scarf that covered the lower part of his face. They were dark eyes, near black and as he took the jewels from her the fine lines at the edges of his eyes deepened, as if he were laughing. Silently she turned and walked back to the coach.

"Villain!" cried Joanna. "I hope you hang for this!"

Without taking his eyes from the carriage the man had remounted his horse, one pistol still levelled at the servants upon the box, the other tucked into his belt.

"No doubt of it m'lady — I shall hang one day — but not just yet, I fancy! Don't think too hardly of Mad Jack — after all you won't be beggared by what I've taken."

"Here's something else to take with you!" said Joanna drawing a small silver-mounted pistol from her muff and taking aim as the rider swung round to ride away. There was a loud report, but even as Mrs Cley squeezed the trigger Caroline gave a groan and collapsed against her in a dead faint, knocking her arm so that the bullet thudded harmlessly into the earth.

* * *

"Well, gentlemen, I think that covers everything. We have discussed this matter pretty well — " Sir Lambert walked across to the fireplace and tugged at the bell-rope. "I suggest we keep to ourselves what has been agreed today. It would seem that this cursed highwayman is being aided by someone locally so the fewer people who know of our plans the better our chances of success."

"When do we begin to patrol the area?" asked Mr Ruthwell.

"It will be full moon next week, so we will start then. We will divide into two groups to take alternate nights — I shall begin on Monday, you, Philip, can take another party Tuesday night."

The major nodded and looked around the room. There were a dozen men there in all, gentlemen farmers and landowners.

"Very well. Simon — you'll come with me? And Flitcomb, Wells and Barnwood — if you are agreeable?"

The gentlemen in question nodded their assent. Mr Ashby gave a nervous cough.

"Hope you don't expect me to join your party, Lagallan. My chest, you know — very weak. I doubt I could endure a prolonged night ride."

He coloured slightly as he met the major's faintly contemptuous eyes.

"I did not really expect you to come with us, Ashby," returned the major coolly.

Sir Lambert looked around at the assembled company.

"If that is all, gentlemen, I think

we may safely leave matters there and turn our attention instead to dinner — nothing special, y'know, my dear lady and I like plain fare, but I've an excellent claret I would like you all to try . . . "

They all rose, ready for their host to lead them to the dining-room, but before Sir Lambert had taken two steps towards the door it flew open and Mrs Cley appeared. Her face was very white and she paused in the doorway, then with a cry she dropped her muff and ran to her brother.

"Simon!" she cried, casting herself upon his chest. "He has struck again! We have been robbed!"

Her words brought a murmur of surprise and indignation from the gentlemen, who gathered around the widow, anxious to hear her tale.

Coming almost unnoticed into the room, Caroline went to a chair at a distance from the main group, thankful for a quiet moment to collect her scattered thoughts. Major Lagallan came over and handed her a glass of wine.

"Are you hurt, Caroline?"

"No — only shaken — please, I am sure you wish to listen to Mrs Cley — I am quite happy to sit here for a while," she assured him and he returned to the group gathered about Mrs Cley.

"Did he offer you violence?" enquired one gentleman.

"He — he threatened us with a pistol — "

"The scoundrel — what did he take?"

Joanna put a hand to one ear.

"My emerald drops — you know the ones, Simon, you gave them to me — "

"Yes, yes. Nothing else?"

She shook her head.

"Caroline gave up a brooch, but it was not very valuable."

"But what of the servants — I specifically told Wedmore to take someone with him, and armed!"

declared Mr Ruthwell angrily.

"It was all so quick — I think the boy dropped his shotgun," explained Joanna, looking perplexed. She clung to her brother. "It was horrible, Simon! He was so rude, so coarse!"

Mr Ruthwell put his arms around her comfortingly.

"There, my dear, it's all over now," he murmured, looking over her head at Sir Lambert.

"I'll question the servants," said the magistrate, "perhaps they can give us some information."

"Can you give us any description, Mrs Cley — anything you remember?" asked Mr Flitcomb.

Joanna shook her head.

"He — he was dressed all in black and had a black horse, but he was masked — I couldn't see his face. Ask Caroline — she was closer to him than I."

Miss Hetton coloured faintly as all eyes turned expectantly towards her.

"I — that is, he was very well

disguised," she stammered.

"How tall was he? Did you note his eyes, or his voice?" Sir Lambert prompted her gently.

"He was quite — short," she decided at last, "and very broad, with a heavy country voice."

"The other reports we've had said he was tall," put in someone.

"He did look taller at a distance," she temporized, adding, "I do not think he intended us any harm."

"Pity Wedmore didn't get a shot at the fellow!" put in Simon, giving his sister's hand a comforting pat.

"But *I* did!" declared Joanna, reviving a little. "I had my own pistol hidden in my muff and I fired at him as he was riding off, but Caroline fainted and spoiled my aim — the chance was lost."

Another murmur rippled through the company.

"Lady Lambert has gone off to visit friends and will not be back until tomorrow," explained Sir Lambert, concern written in his kindly countenance. "If you would care to stay here and take dinner with us I should be delighted, of course, but perhaps you would prefer to go to your own homes?"

Mrs Cley nodded and cast an imploring glance at her brother, who said: "Yes of course. I am sure Sir Lambert will understand if I do not stay."

"Certainly, my dear boy. I expected nothing else. If you will allow me but five minutes to talk to your coachman, Mrs Cley, I shall detain you no longer." He turned to the major. "You too, Philip. I've no doubt you will wish to take Miss Hetton home immediately."

"If Miss Hetton does not object to travelling in an open carriage, I'd be happy to take her home," affirmed the major.

"What of Mr Ashby?" Caroline asked him doubtfully.

"I am sure Sir Lambert would lend Jonas a horse — his chest will survive a short ride, I don't doubt," replied Philip with a ghost of a smile.

Mr Ashby looked uncomfortable, but said nothing and felt compelled to accept his host's assurances that he could find him a very comfortable mount with the best grace he could muster.

The ladies then took their leave, Joanna accompanied by her brother, and Caroline sitting up beside the major in his curricle.

It was almost dark by this time, and although the thick clouds were very high and held no immediate threat of rain, they obscured the gibbous moon that would otherwise have illumined their way. Miss Hetton found the sensation of riding through the gloom in an open carriage not altogether agreeable, and she glanced over her shoulder somewhat nervously. Major Lagallan had not brought his groom with him, and a short distance behind the curricle Caroline could make out the bulky figure of Mr Ashby astride his borrowed horse.

"You need not be afraid of an attack on this stretch of road, Miss Hetton," remarked the major in reassuring accents.

"I am not at all afraid of that," she returned quickly, "that is — I find it rather eerie, to be travelling at night, so exposed to the elements."

"Would you like me to stop and put up the hood for you?"

"Thank you, there is no need," she paused before adding in a strained voice, "I have no doubt you think me very poor-spirited."

"No, why should I?"

"To have fainted off in such a way, when there was never any real danger."

"On the contrary, I think it was very wise of you. Brave, too."

"Oh."

He negotiated a particularly sharp bend in the road before speaking again.

"I wish you would trust me, Caroline."

"Oh, but I do — of course I trust

you!" she replied, much flustered.

"But you will not confide in me."

Caroline shifted uncomfortably.

"Good heavens, sir, *I* have nothing to confide!" she replied with forced lightness. "Perhaps you think I am disillusioned with life at Sandburrows, after today's events — that I pine for my former peaceful existence. I can assure you that is not the case!"

"What I think is that you wilfully misunderstand me, my dear," he returned coolly, "But we will let that pass. I would only beg you to look upon me as your friend."

They had arrived at Lagallan House by this time, and Miss Hetton was spared the necessity of replying. As the curricle came to a stand the door of the house was thrown open and Vivyan came striding out, holding up a lantern.

"At last you are returned!" he declared, walking up to the carriage. "I had expected you a good hour ago, Caroline. When you did not appear at four o'clock we assumed you had stopped to dine with Mrs Cley, but Holly has been fretting for these past two hours, thinking that you might have met with an accident. I told her that if you had stopped at Rhyne House you would not be home early, but I don't mind admitting for the past hour I have been increasing anxious — in fact I was about to ride out looking for you."

"Don't stand there chattering, boy, take Miss Hetton into the house," ordered Mr Ashby, dismounting somewhat shakily from his horse. "The poor young woman's had the devil of a fright and I daresay we would all be the better for a little brandy."

"What's this?" demanded Vivyan, looking closely at Caroline. "Was Holly correct — *has* there been an accident?"

"No, no, nothing of that nature," she assured him as he led her into the house, and looking up into his boyish face she added in an urgent whisper, "I must talk to you, Vivyan! Where have you been today?"

His dark eyes were very bright, she noticed, but his face registered a look of surprise.

"I've been riding my mare on the beach, trying out her paces with Sam Granby, why do you ask?"

Before Caroline could say more, Mrs Hollister appeared and gave a cry of relief when she saw Caroline.

"My dear child I have been near distraught! Come into the drawing-room and tell me what has occurred, you look worn out!"

"Miss Hetton was attacked!" cried Mr Ashby dramatically. "'Twas the self-same rascal who waylaid *me*!"

Major Lagallan ushered them all into the drawing-room and carefully closed the door against the curious stares of the servants.

"You poor child!" exclaimed Mrs Hollister, leading Caroline to an armchair and gently pushing her down into it.

"It would appear that the attack took place close by the Crowsham turning, at the Knoll," explained Major

Lagallan. "No one was hurt, and I believe nothing of great value was taken except a pair of emerald eardrops belonging to Mrs Cley."

"I must say it's not what I expected of you, Lagallan," broke in Mr Ashby testily, "to hear you playing down the incident! Why, man, 'twas only this afternoon you stressed the need to stop the villain, and you were the first to agree with Sir Lambert when he suggested — "

"That's enough." The major did not raise his voice, but it cut through the air like steel and Mr Ashby broke off his speech, looking somewhat indignant.

"The ladies won't wish to hear Sir Lambert's comments, Jonas," continued Major Lagallan coolly. "Let it be sufficient that there are plans afoot to catch the fellow and if he has any sense he will change to some safer occupation."

"I thought these rogues only knew one trade," remarked Vivyan.

"That is true, of course, but for

some unaccountable reason I feel this particular rogue is somewhat different from his brethren of the high toby."

"I understood Mrs Cley was taking an armed guard with her," put in Mrs Hollister, "did she decide otherwise?"

"There was one young lad, Holly, and he was too frightened to be of use, from what I could make out."

"Aye, but what of Mrs Cley?" asked Mr Ashby admiringly, "There's a woman of spirit for you. She wasn't afraid to take on the scoundrel, no ma'am," he continued, turning to Mrs Hollister. "When the fellow was riding away, she fetched out her own little pistol and let fly."

"Goodness!" exclaimed the house-keeper faintly.

Mr Ashby nodded. "Aye, and she'd have got him, too, I believe, if her aim hadn't been spoiled."

"How was that?" enquired Vivyan, standing beside the fireplace, one arm rested negligently along the mantelshelf.

"Miss Hetton swooned at the fatal

moment, and knocked Mrs Cley's hand. Unfortunate, but quite understandable, my dear Miss Hetton," said Mr Ashby, "I pray you don't judge yourself too harshly."

"Did she, by Jove?" murmured Mr Lagallan, his gaze fixed thoughtfully upon Caroline, who looked away, feeling very uncomfortable.

"Now Master Vivyan, you are not to go making the poor child feel any more miserable!" exclaimed Mrs Hollister, observing Caroline's wan complexion. "Because *you* don't have a nerve in your body you cannot expect everyone to be so — I am sure it is a most common thing for one's senses to be temporarily overpowered at such a time." She went across to Caroline and patted her hands. "Try to put it out of your head, my sweet. It is all past now and you are safely back with us. I have some news that will cheer you, I am sure. Mrs Dempster has made up the green silk for you, and it is in your room ready for you to try it on."

"Well if that don't beat all!" exclaimed Mr Ashby. "Here we are with a most desperate villain loose in the district, and all you ladies can think of is a new gown!"

"Not at all," replied Mrs Hollister with gentle dignity. "I am sure we do not underestimate the gravity of the situation, but when one is feeling low, a new gown can achieve miracles in the restoration of one's spirits."

"Perhaps Miss Hetton would care to give us all the pleasure of seeing her in this new creation," suggested the major, a smile in his eyes.

Caroline blushed, giving a shaky laugh.

"I am grateful for the compliment, sir, but after today's adventure my one desire is to sleep!"

"Of course, my dear, how thoughtless we are to keep you talking here," put in Mrs Hollister warmly. "Have you eaten? Would you like me to send up a tray for you?"

"Thank you, that would be very

welcome. I daresay you will think me very poor spirited."

"Not at all, my dear child," cried Mr Ashby, taking her hand and escorting her to the door. "Perhaps I, more than anyone else here, can appreciate what you are suffering at this time, since I too was brutally assaulted! Let me recommend that you try one of Mrs Hollister's powders — I am sure it could do you nothing but good."

Miss Hetton gently but firmly declined all suggestion of medication and escaped to the seclusion of her bedchamber, where she hoped that a little calm reflection and a night's repose would restore her equilibrium.

10

THE next few days passed uneventfully: very little was seen of Vivyan, who left the house before breakfast each morning, returning only for his dinner and a change of clothes before sallying forth once more to join his friends in Crowsham. Mrs Hollister told Caroline that the young master always behaved in this way when his uncle was with them, but Miss Hetton thought that it might be herself that Vivyan wished to avoid. Philip too was busy with the everyday administration of his estate, and joined the ladies only for dinner or to escort them to Crowsham church on Sunday.

★ ★ ★

Monday dawned very grey, and before breakfast was over the rain had set in, steady and relentless, with no sign of letting up for the rest of the day. Assured by Mrs Hollister that no assistance was required for any household duties, Caroline shut herself in the library, resolved to continue her efforts to improve her performance on the pianoforte. She was making good progress at this worthwhile occupation when the major came in. She stopped immediately.

"Do you wish to work in here? I can easily remove — "

"No, I was passing and heard you playing. Please continue." She shook her head, smiling.

"I was trying out the music you were kind enough to purchase, but I am very out of practice, and not at all ready for an audience."

"I thought it sounded very well."

"Thank you, but my fingers are so slow, and seem to be forever tripping over each other! Mr Arne's minuet has been giving me some difficulty, but I am hopeful that a little more practice

176

will make it tolerable."

"I see I have made a grave error in interrupting you — forgive me. I will withdraw and leave you to your music!" he said, a mixture of humour and contrition in his voice.

"Oh no, please — " Caroline rose quickly, saying in a confiding tone: "My dedication is not entirely without its selfish side: I am in part avoiding Mr Ashby. There! I have admitted it, now my conscience may be somewhat clearer!"

"If he has offended you — "

"No, no, it is not so serious as all that," she returned quickly, unsettled by his look of concern. "It is merely that he thinks the unfortunate occurrence on Friday may be turned to his benefit. He tells me it would be no wonder if the hold-up had given me a distaste for Sandburrows and everyone connected with it." She laughed, trying to make light of Mr Ashby's insinuating behaviour, but she knew from the major's countenance that he was displeased.

"If Jonas has been making a nuisance of himself — "

"Oh pray don't allow my ill-considered remarks to cause any unpleasantness. I had no right to speak so of Mr Ashby. After all, it is only natural that he should not welcome your brother's marriage, and in any case his comments are irrelevant, since if I *should* decide to marry Vivyan my home would not be here."

"You have not yet made your decision?"

She began to sort through the sheets of music on the piano.

"'Tis as much your brother's decision, sir. *I* have no other prospect in view, but Vivyan is a very eligible young man, and I am sure he could make a much better match, if he could be persuaded to wait a little."

"And if there were another prospect for you, Miss Hetton, what would be your decision?"

She shook her head at him, a slight

reproachful smile upon her lips.

"Unfair, sir!" she chided him gently. "An impoverished governess dare not allow her imagination free rein. Indeed what could compare with the offer you yourself brought to me in Bath? A comfortable income, secure future and a considerate, and most charming husband."

"A veritable fairytale, in fact."

She was quick to hear the dry note in his voice and all at once it seemed very important to her that he should not despise her.

"Don't think too badly of me, Major," she urged him. "My decision is not an easy one to make. I was not reared to think of money as the only reason for a marriage."

"It is nevertheless a very strong motive," he said quietly.

She met his cool hazel eyes without flinching.

"Certainly."

He came up to her, taking one of her hands in his own strong fingers and raising it to his lips.

"Your honesty does you credit, my dear. You and Vivyan must of course make up your own minds, but you may be assured of one thing. If, for whatever reason, you do not wish to marry my brother, then you may rely upon my full support to ensure that you are taken care of. I will say no more for the present, but I beg that you will bear in mind that I am as concerned for your happiness as for Vivyan's. There need be no marriage if you do not desire it."

"Th — thank you, you are very kind," stammered Caroline, much surprised. She realized her fingers were still caught in his firm clasp, and gently withdrew her hand, turning away from his searching gaze.

"The rain has ceased — I think the sky is at last beginning to clear."

Major Lagallan walked to the window and studied the sky.

"I believe you are right," he said. "I have to ride over to see one of my tenants, Abraham Lee. Would you like to come with me?"

"I should like very much to come — that is, will I not be in the way?"

"Honesty compels me to admit that you will be," he replied gravely. "However, I must consider the other members of my household. I was compelled to utter the first thing that came to mind to save them further experience of your musical abilities!"

Caroline laughed.

"In that case, if you will give me but twenty minutes to change my dress I shall certainly accompany you, and make myself as odious as possible to punish you for that last remark!"

As she hurried to her room she almost collided with Mr Ashby on the stairs. His portly figure stepped to one side, brows raised a little in surprise.

"Your pardon, Miss Hetton. My dear young lady you *are* in a hurry!"

"The major has invited me to ride out with him," she explained cheerfully. "I owe it to my sex to prove to him that we *can* change our attire in less than an hour, when it is necessary!"

Mr Ashby, noting her flushed cheeks and sparkling eyes, silently drew his own conclusions, and stood aside to let her pass.

A ride in the fresh salty air did much to restore Miss Hetton's spirits and after an agreeable evening with Vivyan and his uncle seemingly at pains to be polite to each other, Caroline was led to hope that the remainder of Mr Ashby's stay (and its length had not yet been determined) would pass off relatively peacefully. Alas for such hopes! Tuesday evening saw them dashed. Dinner had gone quietly enough, but Major Lagallan went out shortly after and Caroline recognized that with him went the restraint that had kept uncle and nephew apart. They were drinking tea when matters finally came to a head. Vivyan handed a cup to Caroline and asked for her opinion of his new suit.

"Got my man in Bath to make it

up and he sent it on to me, just arrived today. All the crack in London, y'know. Philip brought the material back with him on his last visit to town, and I had a final fitting in Bath weeks ago, but it has taken the fellow a devil of a time to get it to me."

Caroline thought privately that he looked very well, the dark cloth enhancing his handsome, boyish looks, but before she could frame a reply Mr Ashby broke in, prefixing his remarks with an irritating laugh.

"Goodness, my boy, don't you know better than to ask a young lady for her opinion? What's Miss Hetton supposed to say, eh? Do you expect her to tell you when you're making a cake of yourself?"

"I think Mr Lagallan is looking exceptionally fine," put in Caroline quickly.

Mr Ashby smiled indulgently.

"Aye, well you have to say that now, don't you my dear? Wouldn't do to wound the lad's feelings."

She noticed the shadow of doubt in Vivyan's face at his uncle's words, but in an instant it was concealed.

"Miss Hetton knows she is free to speak as she wishes to me." He cast a scornful glance at his uncle. "Besides, it's about time *you* found yourself a decent tailor, Jonas. All that lace and embroidery has been out of style these ten years."

"Watch you don't spill your tea over Miss Hetton, boy!" commanded Mr Ashby, somewhat unnecessarily, Caroline considered. "P'raps I would get myself rigged out in the latest mode if I wished to impress a female, but a dark pinstripe on a willowy lad like yourself — makes you too lanky by far, boy."

"Mr Ashby is funning, Master Vivyan," said Mrs Hollister, eyeing nervously the angry flush on the younger man's cheek.

"Aye, of course I am!" cried Mr Ashby jovially. "Goodness, lad, you don't take me seriously! What an unaccountable young fellow you are."

"Vivyan, perhaps you would be good enough to give me your advice on what ribbon I should use to trim this bonnet," said Caroline hastily. "I have three pieces here, you see, but I cannot make a decision. Your eye for colour is so good — do you think it should be the *cocquelicot* or the apple green?"

Mr Lagallan responded to her beseeching look and pulled a chair beside Miss Hetton's, muttering under his breath.

"Pray don't let him tease you," murmured Caroline, holding up the ribbons for his inspection.

"If you let him see that you are not affected by his remarks, I am sure he will soon cease."

Vivyan took the ribbons from her and held them up to her cheek, seeming not to have heard her words.

"You should wear the green," he decided at last. "You have green in your eyes — like the grey-green pebbles one sometimes finds on the beach. Strange that I should only now notice it, Philip mentioned it to me when you first arrived."

Caroline blushed.

"He did?"

"Best be careful there, young Vivyan," put in Mr Ashby, "You'll be losing her to your brother."

Vivyan threw him a scornful glance, but his uncle merely chuckled.

"You remind me very much of your Mama when you look down your nose like that!" he mused. "She too could be haughty, when she chose. No strength of will though — pretty little ninnyhammer."

"I'll thank you not to talk of my mother," Vivyan ground out.

"Sorry if it offends you, my boy, but she was m'sister, after all, and I have to admit she was empty-headed — why else would she have left her estate in such a muddle?"

"That's something that needn't worry you much longer, Jonas! I'll have you out of Stanhayes by the end of the year!"

Mr Ashby leaned back in his chair, a condescending smile settling over his chubby features.

"In three months? Am I to understand that you will shortly announce your betrothal?"

"Better than that!" flashed Vivyan. "Caro and I are to be married as soon as it can be arranged — you may be sure it will be within a month."

"Vivyan!" Miss Hetton's bonnet dropped from her nerveless fingers, Mr Ashby's smile was frozen on his face.

"I'm sorry, Caro. I know you didn't want to tell anyone until you had informed your family," said Mr Lagallan, giving her fingers a quick squeeze.

Mrs Hollister looked dazed.

"Is is true?" she asked slowly. "Why such haste, my dears? Surely there is no need — "

"Caroline has been here a month already," explained Vivyan, "but don't worry, Holly. We know what we are about."

"Well well," Mr Ashby tried hard to keep the annoyance from his voice, but did not quite succeed. "So you are desperate for your inheritance, is that it?"

"Nothing of the sort! Caro and I have reached a very good understanding, have we not, my dear?"

Miss Hetton, very pale, nodded silently. Mrs Hollister came over and kissed her cheek.

"Well, I for one am extremely glad to hear it!" she declared, "I think this calls for a special toast. What a pity the major is not here to join in our celebrations, but I am sure he will not object if we ask Stalton to bring us a bottle of the best wine!"

★ ★ ★

Like one in a dream, Caroline listened to the flow of conversation around her and obediently sipped at the glass of wine that was pressed into her hand. Mr Ashby was obviously displeased by what he had heard and took himself off to bed as soon as he had drunk a grudging toast to the happy pair. Mrs Hollister went away soon after, saying with a smile that she expected they would like a little time to themselves, but adjuring Vivyan not to overtire his fiancée.

★ ★ ★

As soon as they were alone, Mr Lagallan put up his hands in a defensive gesture.

"Don't be angry with me, Caro! I know it was wrong of me, but Jonas has been pinching at me for days, now, I could not resist it."

"It was a very foolish thing to do!" replied Miss Hetton, looking grave. "You have put me in a most awkward situation."

"I know I said I would not press you to give me an answer until the end of the month," he said, taking her hands, "but that is little more than a week away now, after all."

"But I have made no decision!" cried Caroline desperately. "And I will not be coerced into marrying you merely to spite your uncle!"

"No, no," he said soothingly. "I would not ask that of you, merely to let matters stand as they are for a while — there is really no need for you to say anything."

"Of course there is a need! You cannot expect me to live out a lie!"

"But don't you *wish* to marry me?"

He looked at her, his face such a mixture of surprise, dismay and almost comic disbelief that she felt her anger evaporating. She continued in a milder tone.

"I have told you, I have not yet made my decision. I do not mean to be missish, or difficult, but marriage is a very big step, and I am not at all sure we should suit."

"No need to worry about that,"

Vivyan told her confidently. "Arranged marriages happen all the time. We shall soon settle into the order of things."

Caroline drew a long breath.

"How can I make you understand? I am a governess, Vivyan. If I do not marry you, all *I* have to look forward to is a series of uninspiring appointments in other people's households; with you it is so very different. Very likely in a year or two you will meet some young lady and fall violently in love with her."

"Devil a bit!" he replied cheerfully. "I've never met a woman yet who could hold my interest for more than a couple of days. Although I'll admit one doesn't see that many females here — " he stopped suddenly, as a new thought struck him. "Caro, I *am* sorry! Is *that* what you want of me, a little more affection? I should have realized that for all your talk of understanding the situation, you would expect a little romantic involvement too — "

"That is not at all what I want, and

if you make any attempt to embrace me at this present moment I shall box your ears!" she replied roundly.

Vivyan had indeed been about to take her in his arms, but at her words he drew back, laughing.

"Very well, Miss Propriety! But what then *do* you want?"

"A little more time to make up my mind."

"But I don't see that a week can make such a difference," argued Vivyan. "You have this minute told me that it is a choice between marrying me and living like a drudge for the rest of your life — I can't see there's anything more to think about."

Caroline recognized the reason of his words and was disinclined to argue further. Sensing this, Mr Lagallan pressed home his advantage.

"Do say you will stand by me, Caro," he said coaxingly. "After all, if you wish to cry off at the end of next week we can arrange something and who knows, perhaps we can persuade

Jonas to take himself off by that time."

They heard a scratching at the door, and Mrs Hollister appeared, saying: "May I come in? I left my workbox here and if I do not put it back in my room you may be sure that by morning one of the servants will have removed it, and then I shall have to hunt high and low for it! It has been an exciting day has it not? I am sure I never expected to hear an announcement from you quite so soon."

Feeling Vivyan's eyes upon her, Caroline merely smiled and she caught his faint sigh of relief as he squeezed her hand.

"Caroline, my dear, you are looking a little tired. It is indeed very late — shall we go upstairs together?"

Miss Hetton acquiesced gracefully, realizing with an inward smile that the good lady had no intention of allowing the young couple to remain alone for too long and had taken upon herself the duties of duenna.

"I — we would be grateful if you

would not tell anyone of — if you would not tell anyone about what has passed this evening, ma'am," said Caroline haltingly, as the two ladies made their way upstairs.

"You may rely upon my discretion," came the warm reply. "It is natural that you should wish to keep the arrangement a secret until your mama has been informed. You may be sure it will not pass my lips outside this house!"

11

IT was borne upon Miss Hetton at breakfast the following morning that however reticent the housekeeper might be when abroad, she was very willing to discuss the forthcoming marriage with members of the Lagallan household.

* * *

Caroline entered the breakfast room as Mrs Hollister was giving Major Lagallan a lively account of the previous night's events, but the good lady broke off the monologue to greet her.

"Good morning, Caroline — I was telling the major of Master Vivyan's announcement yesterday. My dear, I freely admit I had not expected such a sudden decision."

"Miss Hetton has surprised us all,"

remarked the major coolly.

Caroline flushed but said nothing, apparently occupied with her tea and bread and butter.

"I understand you are anxious to marry as soon as possible," Philip continued. "Have you written to your Mama asking her to come here for the occasion? I am sure we have sufficient rooms for any guests you may wish to invite."

"No — that is, we have not yet fixed upon a date," stammered Caroline. "I intend to make my arrangements then."

"Is that not leaving it a little late?"

Hearing the sardonic note in his voice, she was at a loss for a reply and was relieved to see Vivyan in the doorway. He entered, relaxed and cheerful and after a general greeting he hesitated, then stooped to plant a kiss upon Caroline's cheek, and catching her eye he winked at her as he moved away.

"I understand I am to congratulate

you, little brother," said Philip, pouring ale into a mug for Vivyan, and refilling his own.

"That's right. We didn't want to make it known just yet, but Jonas forced it out of me. By the by where is the old trouble-maker?"

"He is taking breakfast in his room," explained Mrs Hollister. "His man told Stalton that Mr Ashby passed an indifferent night, and needs to rest if he is to accompany us to Mr Ruthwell's tonight. I fear the news of Master Vivyan's forthcoming marriage has much displeased him."

"I was under the impression that no decision was to be made until the end of the month," the major fixed an enquiring eye upon his brother, who shifted uncomfortably in his seat.

"Well, that *was* the arrangement, but Caro and I have talked it over and see no need to keep it a secret. Of course," he added, noting Caroline's anguished look, "we don't want it made generally known yet. I know I can rely upon your discretion, Philip."

"Certainly."

Feeling more explanation was needed, Caroline said: "I want to inform my family before any public announcement. It would not do for them to be misinformed."

She looked up to find the major's eyes upon her, amusement clearly written upon his face, and she found herself blushing. In an attempt to change the subject she asked Vivyan if he was going out after breakfast. He nodded.

"I'm riding into Crowsham, do you have an errand for me?"

"You had best take a carriage, Master Vivyan," Mrs Hollister advised him, looking out of the window at the leaden sky. "I fear we will have more heavy rain later. It would be much more sensible if you were to remain at home."

"Can't do that," he said between mouthfuls of ham. "I've promised Sam that I'd meet him at the Viking at noon. He's challenged me to try my bays against a new team his father has just bought him, and we have to arrange a course."

"Would that be the greys Sir Lambert brought here from Huntspill last week?" enquired the major. "From what I saw of them I would say they'll take some beating."

Vivyan was unconcerned.

"They may be good but they won't catch my bays. I've already beaten him once driving back from Weston."

Mrs Hollister looked disapproving.

"Master Vivyan you'll break your neck if you carry on with these races. And you about to be wed, too — the poor child will be widowed almost before she's a bride!"

"Oh Holly, don't be such a goose!" said Vivyan, laughing. "It isn't that risky and besides, a little danger makes life interesting. Of course, when we are married I shall have to give up my racing."

"Will you be back in time to go with us to Simon's?" asked his brother.

"I doubt it. I've already made my apologies to him, so there's no need to worry on that score."

"I wish you would try to come with us," put in Mrs Hollister, "Mr Ruthwell and his sister will be most disappointed."

"No they won't," retorted Vivyan. "If my esteemed uncle is to be one of the party, they will thank Providence that I am staying away. They know how we fight."

"They will not be the only ones to be thankful," remarked Philip dryly. "If you do not come, the rest of us can travel in one carriage, which will save some of my servants from turning out on what promises to be a very wet night!"

* * *

Caroline was pleased to have an occasion to wear the new green silk. She had put it on only once since it had been completed and then only to check that the fit was correct. In her two years as a governess she had grown accustomed to wearing only the most sober colours and she wondered even as she dressed whether this beautiful gown was too extravagant for a quiet country dinner. She mentioned her fears to Mrs Hollister when that lady looked in to see if she was ready.

"Not a bit of it!" the housekeeper reassured her. "I have never seen you looking better. The major has an excellent eye for colour, has he not? The only pity is that Master Vivyan is not here to see you. However, you must not be discouraged if Mrs Cley is wearing another of her London gowns and outshines us all. She invariably does so!"

★ ★ ★

The rain did not let up, but neither did it prevent any of the guests from reaching Rhyne House. Major Lagallan's party was the last to arrive, and as

Caroline and Mrs Hollister entered the drawingroom after discarding their outer garments and rearranging their curls, they were not at all surprised to find the main subject of conversation was the weather. It was not a large gathering, and Miss Hetton was acquainted with everyone present, with the exception of one middle-aged couple who were presently introduced to her as Mr and Mrs Thirsby. She recognized Mr Joseph Thirsby, their son, and was faintly surprised that he was not with Vivyan and his friends at the Viking, but supposed that he had been compelled by filial obedience to attend the party with his parents.

Caroline chose a vacant seat close to Lady Granby, who said as she approached: "I am so glad you could come, Miss Hetton. I very much feared this persistent rain would turn the evening sadly flat, but everyone is here, except for Vivyan, who I understand has a prior engagement, and my own dear Sir Lambert, who is obliged to go out — such a dreadful night too! It is not generally known," she added, lowering her voice, "but he has got up a party and is searching for our local highwayman. What he expects to find on a night like this I don't know, and so I told him, but there, he says 'tis his duty, and must be done, but he insisted Samuel should come in his place, not liking to have Fanny and myself travelling the lanes at night with only servants to attend us."

"Your son is here?" broke in Caroline, startled, "But I thought — "

"He is upstairs in one of the guest rooms," replied his fond mama, her eyes twinkling merrily. "He could not be persuaded to squeeze into the chaise with us, but insisted upon riding and of course the damp has wilted his shirt points and quite ruined the perfect folds of his cravat! The poor boy is even now trying to repair the damage!"

Miss Hetton managed to reply in kind, but her eyes searched the room for Major Lagallan. A terrible foreboding had come over her and she was a little surprised that the major should be her first and only choice as confidant. However, private speech was impossible for the moment: he was talking to Mrs Cley and a pause for reflection caused Caroline to shrink from voicing what was after all only a suspicion. Instead she tried to concentrate upon what Lady Granby was saying to her and made a valiant effort to appear untroubled.

Across the room, the major had seen her anxious look and was thoughtful. Mrs Cley was close beside him, looking very beautiful in cream flowered silk.

"I am so pleased *you* did not cry off tonight," she said softly. "I was terrified the weather would keep you away, and I went to such pains to look my best."

"You need not have worried. There is little chance of the roads becoming impassable tonight, although if the rain continues there is a possibility of flooding with the spring tide later this week."

Mrs Cley found this reply most unsatisfactory. She pouted prettily and tapped his arm playfully with her fan.

"You know that is not the answer I wished to hear, you tiresome creature!" she admonished him, "You are supposed now to compliment me upon my gown or notice the new way I have of dressing my hair."

The major raised her hand to his lips.

"As always you are looking very beautiful, Joanna."

Mrs Cley was unused to receiving anything less than a gentleman's full attention, but she curbed her impatience, and tried instead a different line.

"I have today received a letter from Lady Mountford — perhaps you have met her in London?"

"I do not recall having had that honour."

"But you *have* met her son, Penlan. He came down here in the spring to stay with Simon."

He inclined his head.

"A very amiable gentleman, as I remember."

"Yes, very charming," returned Joanna, watching him carefully. "He was *most* attentive to me when we met in town and now his mama has invited me to visit her."

If she expected some show of concern or jealousy in the major, Joanna was disappointed: his countenance expressed only mild interest and she allowed the matter to drop, moving away shortly after to talk to some of her brother's other guests. She did not speak to Major Lagallan again until they were seated together at the dinner table. Conversation flowed as freely as the wine, and both helped to cut out the sound of the rain which fell unremittingly upon the windows.

After dinner the ladies returned to the drawing-room on the first floor, where candles had been lighted and curtains pulled against the unfriendly night. Talk became desultory, only the three older ladies seeming not to miss the menfolk for they settled down to enjoy a lively discussion of their favourite remedies, including a cure for ague made from agrimony and honey, which Mrs Thirsby claimed to have personal knowledge of its success. Mrs Cley took up a copy of *The New Lady's Magazine* and flicked idly through the pages, leaving Caroline and Miss Granby to amuse themselves as best they could. Miss Granby made a valiant effort to overcome her shyness and responded eagerly to her companion's attempts at conversation, even introducing several topics herself. Their discussion showed little sign of flagging, but when they touched upon the subject of music, they were soon interrupted by Mrs Cley.

"Tell me, Miss Hetton," she said in a loud, carrying tone, "Is there not a fine pianoforte at Stanhayes?"

"I cannot tell you," returned Caroline, mildly surprised, "I have never been there."

"Oh, but surely Mr Lagallan has described it to you? After all, if the reports I have heard are true, he will shortly be making Stanhayes his home."

There was no mistaking the knowing look, but Miss Hetton tried to answer coolly.

"You must ask Mr Lagallan himself, ma'am, since I have no answer for you."

Mrs Cley gave a soft laugh.

"Have I offended you? I am sorry for it and accept the rebuke. I should know better than to listen to servants' tattle, but life is so dull here one must needs take what pleasure one can — " she broke off as a loud insistent knocking was heard from below. "Who can that be at the door at this time of night?"

Lady Granby, who had been listening intently, stood up suddenly and went to the door.

"Mayhap it is Sir Lambert," she said, her face full of concern. "Forgive me, Joanna, if I appear excessively forward, but I must go to see — "

Mrs Cley jumped up.

"I too want to know what is going on!" she declared, following Lady Granby out of the room. After the briefest hesitation the remaining ladies followed suit. The double doors of the drawing-room opened on to the landing not far from the staircase leading down into the entrance hall. When the ladies reached the stairs they found the gentlemen already come out from the dining-room and gathered about a great-coated figure whose shoulders gleamed wet with rain.

"My dear Sir Lambert!" cried Mrs Cley, hurrying down the stairs. "Why ever are you standing here, the servants should have brought you upstairs — "

The magistrate sketched her a bow.

"Servant, Mrs Cley, I would not come further into the house in muddied boots and dripping with rain. In any event I cannot stop, my party waits in your stableyard for me."

"The highwayman — you have caught him?" asked Lady Lambert, coming up to her husband.

He shook his head.

"Nay, almost! We were patrolling the old Bristol road when we came slap upon the fellow about to take another coach!"

"What happened then?" asked Mr Ashby eagerly. "Did the fellow make a run for it?"

"Aye. We got pretty close before he was aware of us, but that horse of his gave him the hint, must have got our scent and the villain got away, blast him! He took a bullet with him, though, which will slow him down. That's why I called in here, to tell you all to check your outbuildings with care for the next few days. The fellow will need somewhere to hide out — he can't travel far with a bullet in him. I don't doubt we'll have him soon enough."

"Where do you go now? Shall we come with you?"

"No need, Simon, thank you. We lost his trail a mile or so back and in this rain there's little chance of finding it again, but we will carry on for a while. What I propose is to make a thorough search as soon as it is light, so perhaps you can all come to the Court tomorrow morning."

There was a murmur of assent and Sir Lambert strode off to rejoin his party of riders. The others watched him go, a sense of excitement in the air, but a strangled cry brought their attention quickly to the staircase. Mrs Hollister gave a shriek.

"Caroline, my dear! Are you hurt?"

"My ankle — " whispered Caroline.

The major came forward and ignoring Miss Hetton's protests he moved aside her skirts and ran his fingers carefully over the suspect joint.

"Can you move your foot?"

"I — I do not think — Oh!"

"Is it broken?" asked Mrs Hollister, "The poor child is so white."

"No, I don't think there are any bones broken, but it is badly sprained. Don't try to get up, child. If you would order the carriage, Simon, Miss Hetton had best be taken home at once."

"Yes of course!" exclaimed Mrs Hollister. "We must go home immediately. Poor Caroline, does it pain dreadfully?"

"There is no need for anyone to come with me," murmured Caroline, "I would much prefer you to stay and enjoy yourselves. I am sure the major would not object if his servants returned for you after supper."

Mrs Hollister threw up her hands in horror.

"My dear girl how can you think I could enjoy myself while you are so poorly? Of course we must all go now, I am sure Mrs Cley will understand . . . "

"In this instance I am afraid I must agree with Miss Hetton," put in the major, who was still kneeling beside the young lady. "It would be best if Miss Hetton travelled with her foot up, and that would mean taking up one side of the coach, and one of us would have to ride." He paused, looking up at Mr Ashby, who blenched visibly at the thought of riding through the torrential rain that could still be heard beating down. "I think it would be best if I return now with Miss Hetton and I will send the coach back for you, Ashby, to escort Mrs Hollister to Lagallan House after supper."

"Why not stay here? There is no need for you to travel tonight," put in Mrs Cley, "I will have Doctor Jeffrey ride here from Weston at first light."

"That is very kind of you, Joanna, but we will not put you to such trouble. All Miss Hetton needs is a good night's rest in her own room and if her ankle is no worse, she will not need to see a doctor, merely to have the ankle strapped up for a few days. I think that is the coach at the door now. If someone will fetch Miss Hetton's cloak and my coat, we will be on our way."

12

MISS HETTON made no protest as the major picked her up and carried her out to the waiting coach, where he set her down, none too gently, upon the seat. He did not speak until the carriage was on its way, lumbering through the dark lanes with the wind buffeting them, and throwing the rain against the side of the coach.

"How is your ankle now?"

"I — I believe it is not quite so serious as I feared," she replied cautiously.

"Then you have fared better than you deserve. What a muddle-headed thing to do!"

"If it comes to that, it was very unkind of you to pinch my leg as you did!" she retorted, nettled.

In the darkness she saw his teeth gleam.

"Convinced everyone you were really hurt, didn't it? But I hope you will have more sense than to try such a thing again. You could have been seriously injured, throwing yourself downstairs in such a fashion. However, I must not rail at you too much, since it provided me with the perfect excuse I needed to go home and see what can be done for my headstrong brother."

Caroline gave a gasp.

"You know?"

"Rather I have guessed. Since his mama died I have feared that he might do something wild. How did *you* find out?"

"It was only a suspicion," she said quickly, "there have been so many coincidences — too many — even now I hope I may be proved wrong."

"I very much doubt it." He paused, then said quietly, "Why did you not come to me with your fears?"

"How could I?" she uttered, distress in her voice, "I had no proof — it would have been unforgivable of me to suggest that Vivyan might be capable of highway robbery! What if my fears had been groundless?"

"Alas it seems they are to be realized," he replied. "What a ridiculous tangle! God knows I have tried to talk to Viv about it, but I cannot get close to him — he craves excitement, Sandburrows is far too quiet for him. If I can extricate him from this mess I'll see what I can do for him, perhaps buy him a pair of colours."

"I had thought he was promised to stay here until he came into his inheritance — did he not vow to his mama to do so?"

"If he does remain here it could very well cost him his life! No, I'll override that oath if I have to, but let us take one step at a time, and the first is to find the boy and see what state he is in."

The carriage had come to a stand, and the major once more lifted her into his arms.

"We must carry through this little

charade," he remarked as he stepped down from the carriage, carrying her easily in his arms, and striding past the astonished servants up the stairs to Caroline's chamber.

"Miss Hetton has sprained her ankle," he explained to the maid who watched open-mouthed as Miss Hetton was laid carefully upon the day-bed. Then, with a slight bow, Major Lagallan turned and left the room.

The major made his way directly to his brother's apartments on the far side of the house. His knock brought Vivyan's man to the door, looking distinctly worried.

"Evening, Dolton, I have come to see my brother," he said, walking past the valet, who made a half-hearted attempt to deny him entry. Major Lagallan strode through the small ante-chamber into the bedroom beyond and there, sitting at a small table with a pile of bloody bandages on the floor beside him, was Vivyan. His face was very pale, the dark eyes feverishly bright. He had removed his coat and shirt and with his left hand he held a wad of cloth to his right arm, just below the shoulder. Without a word Philip went across and took the cloth from the fingers which trembled slightly. He inspected the wound carefully.

"You were lucky," he remarked coolly. "The bullet has barely grazed the arm. You will be in pain for a couple of days, but I see no need to call a surgeon."

"What are you doing here, Philip? Did Bell tell you about me?" demanded Vivyan suspiciously.

Philip was busy binding the wound and did not answer immediately.

"Granby called in at Simon's, told us his patrol had winged their man. I guessed you might need help."

Vivyan raised a quizzical eyebrow.

"What, no reproaches, big brother? I thought you'd be mightily annoyed if you knew I'd taken to the high toby."

The major finished knotting the

bandage and helped Vivyan to put on his nightshirt.

"Too late for that," he said quietly.

He turned to the valet, hovering anxiously about them.

"Can you dispose of these?" he asked, pointing to the soiled dressings and Vivyan's bloodstained clothes. "They'll need to be destroyed, and without any of the other servants being involved."

"Take 'em to Bell," ordered Vivyan, "he'll know how to do the thing, and bring me up a bottle of brandy. I've the devil of a headache."

Philip picked up a half-filled glass that stood on the table.

"What's this?"

"Laudanum, sir, but Mr Vivyan refuses to take it," explained the valet woodenly.

Philip held out the glass.

"Drink it, little brother, or I'll force it down your throat," he said cheerfully.

Vivyan eyed him indignantly, but with a shrug he took the glass and drained it. When the valet had withdrawn,

Major Lagallan helped Vivyan into bed, where he lay back against the pillows, his face pale and drawn.

"I'm grateful to you, Philip," he said at last.

"Save your thanks until you are out of this business," the major advised him gently.

"Does anyone else know about this?"

"No-one except Miss Hetton."

Vivyan frowned.

"Damn you, Phil, I won't have you discussing my affairs with my fiancée."

"I did not tell her, if that is what you are thinking. She guessed at the truth and told me so on the way back here tonight. By the by, *is* she your fiancée?" he asked casually. "I had the oddest fancy that you had thought that one up to confound Jonas."

"Well, if Caro knows about this little episode I doubt she will wish to marry me now." He winced as a stab of pain shot through him as he tried to sit up, and he sank back again, his face as white as the pillow behind his head.

"Lie still, boy," Philip advised him, gently brushing a strand of dark hair from his brow. "From what I've seen of the young lady I don't think this will make her cry off. As soon as she heard Sir Lambert's tale of having wounded 'Mad Jack', she wanted to come to your aid — threw herself down the stairs at Rhyne House just to have an excuse to return here."

Vivyan's eyelids were dropping as the laudanum took its effect, but he managed the ghost of a smile."

"Did she, by Jove? Wonderful girl, ain't she? Deserves better than I can give her."

"Yes. She's a most unusual young lady."

Under his brother's watchful eyes, Vivyan slipped away into sleep, his breathing steadied into a deep, regular pattern. Dolton, entering quietly with a decanter in one hand, found the major sitting at the bedside, thoughtfully regarding his brother. At the sight of the still form in the bed the valet cast a frightened look at Major Lagallan.

"Merciful Heavens, is he — ?"

"He is sleeping," said the major, getting up. "Call me if he wakes in the night, or shows any sign of fever. And try to keep that away from him," he added, pointing to the decanter. "At least for a couple of days."

The major was somewhat relieved to receive no summons to attend his brother in the middle of the night, and at dawn he set off to join Sir Lambert in his search for the highwayman. As he expected, they found no clues, and while some of the gentlemen were exclaiming that the fellow had disappeared from the face of the earth, Philip was silently praising his brother's presence of mind in covering his tracks so well. He returned to Lagallan House in time for breakfast, after which he slipped away to Vivyan's room, where he found the wounded party propped up on his pillows, indulging in a hearty repast.

"Morning, Philip," he said cheerfully.

"You look surprised: did you expect to find me at death's door?"

"I confess I thought to find you with a high fever. How is the arm?"

Vivyan pulled a wry face.

"Hellish! Dolton had a look at it this morning and said it's clean enough, but it's damned sore!"

"Serves you right, you young hot-head!" retorted Philip affably, adding, as his eyes fell upon the breakfast dishes. "Are you sure you should be eating all that?"

"Lord yes! The only problem is that I can't use my right hand. Dolton had to cut everything in pieces for me." He speared a final piece of cold beef and signalled to his man to remove the tray. "What now, big brother," he continued when they were alone, "have you come to comb my hair for me?"

"Not really. I would like to know why you've been acting like a common thief these past months."

Vivyan stared past him towards the window, his eyes dark and intense.

"In truth I cannot tell you. Boredom, I suppose. I thought it would be exciting to kick up a lark, and after I'd done it once it seemed so easy to carry on."

"Where did you acquire the horse? It's not from these stables."

"No. Bell bought her for me at Bridgwater and brought her up — rode her cross-country to avoid curious eyes. Beautiful mare, part Arab, you know, but very big and powerful. She's stabled with a farmer on the Knoll. I pay him well to keep quiet."

"Have you ever considered that it might cost the fellow dear if it is discovered that he has a highwayman's nag in his stable?" asked the major casually.

The boy flushed.

"I don't see that — after all it ain't his horse, and in any case no-one's been killed or even wounded — except me, and I don't *keep* anything."

"Yes, I wondered why you had been so clumsy as to let Sir Lambert's men find your hide-out."

Vivyan grinned.

"I set it up for 'em!" he chuckled. "Led them a merry dance and finally made it seem that I'd been forced to flee at a minute's notice, leaving my booty behind me! I was planning to do the same with the latest prizes — I've got Joanna's earrings to return, you know." He glanced up enquiringly at Philip. "I don't suppose you'd like to take over for me for a few days? Keep 'em guessing."

The major laughed.

"In no way! But I will do my best to help you out of this, if you will do as I say."

"Does that mean giving up the high toby?"

"Yes."

"And if I refuse?"

"I don't think you can. Without help you will be caught within the week."

"Are you telling me that you will hand me over to Sir Lambert?"

Philip shook his head.

"It wouldn't be necessary. Jonas is suspicious of you, you know. He was asking questions about you at breakfast, and it is only a matter of time before he takes his suspicions to Crowsham Court. After all, he has everything to gain from your conviction."

He paused to let the words sink in, watching Vivyan's face as it mirrored his changing emotions.

"Very well. What do you want me to do?"

"First, your groom must get rid of the mare — take her out of the area and sell her. Tell me where you've hidden everything you have stolen and not yet returned — I'll see to it that it is unearthed by someone of unimpeachable honesty. Then we must get you on your feet again and allay any suspicions."

Vivyan sank back on his pillows, his handsome, boyish face very grey.

"Tell Bell what you want him to do with the mare — he'll know best how to set about it, and he'll be thankful, too. He's never been in favour of my 'hobby'."

"And the stolen property?"

Vivyan's tired eyes danced.

"Hidden in the library. Do you remember the secret compartment you showed me when we were boys — behind the panelling beside the fireplace? I thought it would be as good a place as any. Caroline caught me coming out of the library one night when you were at Bristol. Thought I'd had it then, but managed to convince her I had merely been out riding and found myself locked out."

The major stood up.

"Pity you had not been so innocently engaged! I will do what I can for you. By the by, I have set it about that you came home very drunk last night, which is why you are still in your room, but if you can get dressed and show yourself to the servants today, it will help. I'll come back and see you later, and we will discuss what next is to be done."

"I would have thought that was obvious," put in Vivyan tersely. "I shall marry Caroline, if she will have me, and live like some honest country squire for the rest of my days."

"I think not. I had it in mind that you might like a pair of colours — you would probably want a cavalry regiment, would you not?"

For a brief moment Vivyan looked interested, then his mouth set in a stubborn line and he shook his head.

"No, you won't persuade me to it, Philip. Caroline's had a pretty rough time of it up to now and I won't fob her off — dammit you surely don't expect me to tell her it's all off, knowing that all she has to go back to is a life that's little better than a servant's! I'll not do it. If she will have me I'll marry her and settle down. I may not be the best of husbands, but I'll try my best to make her happy!"

Philip saw he was looking tired and merely smiled, saying gently: "We will discuss it when you are feeling better, boy. I think you should try and rest again now."

He slipped cautiously out of the apartment, taking care to avoid being seen and set off in search of Miss Hetton. He found her in the drawing-room, reclining on a couch with a small table at her side, littered with books and magazines thoughtfully provided by Mrs Hollister.

"I am glad you have come," she told him, smiling. "I was sure you would, as soon as you were free to do so without attracting undue attention."

"You seem to understand the situation very well," he replied, pulling a chair near to the couch. "You have been extremely patient."

"I may have *appeared* composed when I limped into the breakfast room this morning, but let me assure you that I have not slept all night, and my brain is *seething* with questions! I pray you will tell me everything."

He gave her a reassuring assessment of his brother's injury, and a brief outline of his plans.

"If we can convince everyone that Vivyan is fit and well, then perhaps fake an accident in a day or so to account for the stiffness in his right arm, I think we can carry the thing off."

Caroline looked thoughtful.

"Is it possible, then, to extricate him?" she asked slowly. "I know it is high spirits that brought Vivyan to this pass, but the penalties are fearful . . . "

"The boy is making a good recovery and he is not lacking in spirit. Unless he does something very foolish I believe we can pull him through this mess."

"But there is a risk," pursued Caroline, looking up at him anxiously, "not least to yourself. Do you think, if you were to talk to Sir Lambert, something could be done? After all, as you have said, nothing has *really* been stolen — "

He shook his head.

"I admit I do not like to deceive such a good friend as Sir Lambert, but I cannot involve him in this — if he knew the truth he would be bound by duty to arrest Vivyan. No, I shall manage this as best I can. I have no right to ask it, but your help would be very welcome."

"Of course!" she declared, giving him her hands. "You cannot doubt I will do everything I can."

He kissed her fingers.

"I thought as much. Thank you, my dear."

13

THE major was engaged to dine with Mr Ruthwell and his sister, before joining the rest of the gentlemen who were to resume the search for the high-wayman. Arriving at Rhyne House, he was shown into the morning room where he found Mrs Cley, alone.

"Philip, my dear!" she rose to greet him, her hands held out. "Simon has been delayed and is only now gone up to his room, so I am afraid you have only myself to entertain you."

"I am sure you will do so charmingly, as usual, Joanna."

She sat down again, patting the sofa beside her invitingly.

"How do matters go on at the Hall, is Miss Hetton recovered from her fall?"

"Very nearly," he replied, sitting

beside her. "I believe her ankle still pains her a little, but she bears it cheerfully enough and does not complain."

"I can well believe it. She is a very — *retiring* — type of person, I would say, and not one to want to draw attention to herself."

"Indeed not. A most unassuming young lady."

She stole a glance at him under her long lashes.

"I have heard it said that she is come to marry Vivyan. Is that true, Philip?"

He smiled faintly.

"That is something you must ask Miss Hetton or my brother, Joanna. I have no reliable information upon that head."

She pouted.

"I am sure you know more than you will say. Will you not confide in me a little?" she said coaxingly, "We are, after all, such *good* friends, are we not?"

Still he smiled, but said nothing and

after a moment she gave a faint sigh and leaned back upon the sofa.

"I will not press you further, for I can see it would prove useless."

"Quite."

"You are horridly unco-operative! Instead I shall tell you of my own concerns! You may recall I mentioned to you yesterday the kind invitation I have received from Lady Mountford?"

He inclined his head and she continued, gazing down thoughtfully at the diamond rings that adorned her slender fingers.

"I have been trying all day to decide if I should accept. We have known each other for a long time now, Philip, and I trust your judgement. Can you advise me what to do?"

"I see no reason why you should not accept."

"But could it not be misconstrued?" she asked him, a faint blush colouring her cheek. "Might not her son think that I had come because I particularly wished to see him?"

234

"Would that be the truth?"

She rose, her usual self-assurance abated as she took a turn about the room.

"I do not know! Certainly I would be pleased to see Penlan again; I find him a most charming companion, but — " she hesitated, then came quickly across the room to sit once more beside the major. "Let me be honest with you, dear Philip! I have been a widow these past three years and have little taste for the state. I am not yet nine and twenty, and I know many people consider me beautiful, so I do not despair of marrying again, yet I would not wish to raise false hopes in any man's heart. If Penlan were to make me an offer, what should I tell him?"

"You look to me for your answer?"

For a long moment their eyes met, then Joanna's gaze fell. She said softly: "I will not deny I have used every charm upon you, Philip, apparently without effect and have now come perilously close to declaring myself."

"Not quite without effect, my dear, I assure you."

"At first I thought I had in some measure gained your affection, but of late — " she gave a tiny laugh. "I begin to think that your heart is engaged elsewhere."

He did not reply, but what she read in his eyes told her enough. With a tiny sigh she rose again and moved away.

"I think you have given me my answer, sir," she said lightly. "Tomorrow I shall write to Lady Mountford accepting her invitation. After all, Penlan is exceedingly rich, and heir to vast estates. He is also very fond of town life."

Philip smiled. "Then the gentleman has the advantage. I am notorious for my love of this area. I wish you may achieve your happiness, my dear."

She stepped across to him and reaching up, kissed him lightly.

"Indeed sir, I think I have a very good chance of doing so! You have solved most of my problems for me and

I wish I could do something in return, though Heaven knows you are always too well organized to need anyone's help!"

She stepped away as the door opened, Mr Ruthwell entered with apologies for his late appearance. The major returned a suitable reply and the conversation turned naturally to more everyday concerns.

* * *

At Lagallan House, dinner was a subdued affair with only Mrs Hollister, Caroline and Mr Ashby there to amuse one another, Stalton having informed them that Master Vivyan had driven out some hours previously with no intention of returning until late. Left to themselves, the ladies might well have spent a peaceful evening catching up with the mending of the household linen, which task Mrs Hollister set herself at this time each year, but Mr Ashby declared that with a wounded and dangerous villain on the loose he was not going to leave them unattended, at least until Philip returned. He was clearly uneasy about the thought of a desperate fugitive bursting in upon them and personally checked that all the ground floor windows were secured as darkness closed in. Mrs Hollister and Caroline were inclined to laugh at his antics, but when Mr Ashby produced a loaded pistol from his pocket, with the intention of keeping it by him all evening, Mrs Hollister called a halt and demanded that he remove the fearsome weapon immediately. Mr Ashby did so, but reluctantly, and seemed set to spend the remainder of the evening pacing the room. He could not be persuaded to retire and in desperation Mrs Hollister produced a pack of cards and suggested they play a few friendly games. This succeeded very well, apart from a startled jerk from Mr Ashby when Stalton brought in the tea tray.

It was just before midnight when

a commotion in the hallway drew their attention. Ignoring Mr Ashby's warnings to be careful, Miss Hetton walked out into the entrance hall, her two companions close behind her. The scene that met their eyes was not in the least bit menacing. An outraged Stalton stood in the doorway, a branched candle-stick held aloft to illuminate Major Lagallan and his brother, who was leaning heavily against him and muttering disjointed sentences into the major's greatcoat. Philip looked up and saw the little group.

"I am sorry you should witness such a scene," he addressed them gravely, displeasure writ large upon his countenance. "I came upon Vivyan in the lane not far from here, almost senseless and his groom endeavouring to drive the bays and stop the boy from toppling out into the road."

Vivyan raised his head and peered across the hall, blinking owlishly.

"Evenin' ladies," he said at last, his speech slurred and slow. "Hello

Jonas! Why wasn't you out with Philip, helping him to catch our villain — no stomach for it, eh?"

"More to the point, why weren't you?" retorted Mr Ashby, his round face flushed and indignant. "Bah! The boy's dead drunk, I can smell the spirits from here! A fine display of conduct, I must say, and the lad not yet twenty!"

"Any luck with your search, Major?" enquired Mrs Hollister.

"A small success. We found more of the property he'd stolen. Simon found it under a hedge not far from Rook's Bridge. It would appear the fellow hid it there after he was wounded on Wednesday, there were bloodstains on the saddlebag. Granby has posted a look-out nearby in case the fellow returns to retrieve it, and he's taken everything back to Crowsham Court to be noted and returned to its rightful owners."

As he was speaking, Caroline was anxiously watching Vivyan, whose eyes were closing and opening as if he was fighting to remain conscious. It was very hard to see in the dim light, but she thought she could detect a dark stain spreading over the arm of his coat.

"I think, Major," she interrupted him, her voice full of outraged dignity, "you had best get your brother to his room. He is looking decidedly unwell. I am sure we have all had enough of his unpleasant behaviour!"

"Very true, Miss Hetton," Philip agreed. "I am sure he will offer you his own apologies tomorrow when he is in a fit state to do so, but for now please accept my profound regret that you should see him like this."

With these words, he took a firmer grip upon Vivyan and half-carried the boy up the stairs.

14

"I MUST say I am not at all surprised to see my nephew is absent this morning."

Mr Ashby made his remark as he took his seat at the breakfast table the morning after Vivyan's ignominious home-coming. It was addressed to no-one in particular and the assembled company, Mrs Hollister, Miss Hetton and the major, all ignored it. Nothing daunted, Mr Ashby continued to anim-advert upon over-indulgence by the young, and the dangers of allowing immature persons too much licence. No-one attempted to check this flow of eloquence, but each made haste to escape from the room; the major to an interview with one of his tenant farmers, Mrs Hollister to her linen-room and Caroline, lacking any other employment, to her room to write up her journal. Since she was far too cautious to commit any of the present intrigue to paper, this was soon completed and she made her way to the landing, intent upon finding her tambour frame, which she thought she had left downstairs.

As she reached the top of the stairs, she saw someone kneeling down at the foot of the staircase, inspecting the carpet. A second glance revealed that it was Mr Ashby. Caroline drew back a little, unsure what to do, and even as she paused, he called to the butler who was crossing the hall.

"What do you make of this, Stalton? There's a stain here, on the carpet."

"Indeed, sir?" replied Stalton woodenly. "Perhaps one of the maids has spilled some wine there. I will enquire."

"No, I don't think that's it," replied Mr Ashby, taking another close look. "It's more like blood — quite recent too, it has not yet been walked into the pile."

The butler's eyebrows rose in mild astonishment.

"Blood sir? I cannot think how it got there! I will have it cleaned immediately . . ."

"No, no, don't do that! Rather make sure it is *not* touched. By the by, did you see Mr Lagallan yesterday morning?"

"Yes sir. He went out about noon."

"And was there anything — odd about him?"

"Odd sir?"

"Yes — did he walk stiffly, or carry himself as though he had sustained an injury?"

Stalton slowly shook his head.

"Not at all. He walked out of here, climbed into his carriage and drove off, as is his custom."

"And where is Mr Lagallan now?"

"Still in his room, I believe."

Mr Ashby began to ascend the stairs, sparing only a cursory nod for Miss Hetton as he passed her.

Stalton was still looking thoughtful when Caroline came downstairs, and a casual enquiry from her brought the information that Major Lagallan was still engaged with one of his tenants. Miss Hetton was about to walk away, but a slight cough from the butler made her pause.

"Yes, Stalton. What is it?"

"I hope you will forgive the impertinence, Miss, but I am a little concerned that the gentleman should be asking so many questions about Mr Vivyan." He looked a little embarrassed, but continued: "There's a lot of gossip about at the moment, you see, with all these robberies and the like, it makes one suspicious and it occurs to me that maybe the major should be informed that such questions are being asked."

Caroline had been wondering how best she could achieve a private word with Philip for just this purpose and Stalton's suggestion found instant favour with her.

"Yes, yes," she agreed warmly. "I think it *most* important that he should be told, and at the earliest possible opportunity."

She would have continued into the drawing-room, but a voice from above made her halt.

"Oh Caroline my dear, are you busy? I am desperate for your help!" Mrs Hollister leaned over the landing balustrade. "I am trying to finish my inventory of the linen and the only girl who is free to help me cannot write *or* reckon! Could you come up and help me? I am anxious to get it finished today."

"Of course," said Caroline, immediately turning about. "I shall be pleased to assist you."

She accompanied the housekeeper to the linen room, silently praying that Stalton would soon find an opportunity to inform the major of Mr Ashby's behaviour.

★ ★ ★

Entering his brother's bedroom, Major Lagallan found Vivyan sitting on the side of the bed, his waistcoat unbuttoned, and his chin pointing to the ceiling while Dolton busied himself with the folds of the neckcloth. Realizing the extreme delicacy of this operation, the major made himself comfortable in an armchair and watched in silence as the servant completed his task. At last he stepped back: slowly Mr Lagallan lowered his head to a more normal position and stared long and hard into the hand-mirror that Dolton held before him.

"Yes," said Vivyan at last. "It will do. Now do up these buttons for me, there's a good fellow. Hello, Philip, do you want to talk to me?"

"I do, but there is no hurry. Finish dressing first. You intend to go out?"

"Yes. I'm meeting Sam and Joseph — we have arranged to hold our race today, although they have neither of 'em any chance against me. I was afraid I might have to cry off, but I'm feeling very much better today, thank God! I only wish this confounded rain would stop."

"Do you really intend to race those bays?" asked Philip, frowning, "Your arm is still far from mended."

Vivyan did not reply immediately, but concentrated on getting his coat on with the minimum of discomfort. At last it was done, and after a final straightening of a seam and smoothing out of a crease, Dolton left the room, satisfied that his master's appearance would not discredit him.

"I know how concerned you were when it opened up again last night," said Vivyan, studying his reflection in a long glass. "I assure you Dolton has bandaged it exceeding well today. Once outside the house I need not use my right hand much at all."

"It may be too late for that," replied the major. "Ashby spotted a bloodstain on the carpet this morning and has been asking a number of searching questions."

"Oh has he? Perhaps that's why he made such a determined effort to get in here a while ago."

"And did he succeed?"

Vivyan grinned.

"No. He made it as far as that door, Dolton telling him all the time that I was indisposed, but when he started to come in here I told him if he dared to come disturbing my peace after such a night as I had endured, I would blow his head off. It seemed to do the trick, for he went off again immediately."

"Yes," agreed the major grimly. "I believe he has gone to Crowsham Court to see Sir Lambert."

Vivyan stared at his brother.

"You cannot be serious!"

"Never more so. He has no cause to love you and he has been suspicious for quite a while, I think. The bloodstain in the hall strengthened his suspicions, and no doubt your refusal to see him confirmed them. We've got to act, and quickly."

Vivyan sat down again on the edge of the bed.

"What do you propose, Philip?"

"We will think up some plausible

tale to account for the stain — one
of my dogs bringing in a rabbit or
some such thing — then if we can
convince Granby that Jonas has allowed
his baser instincts to lead him to a
false conclusion, we may still carry
it off. Granby knows enough of how
things stand between you and Jonas
to believe such a thing is possible.
The most important thing now is to
arrange for your — ah — accident.
It is important that as few people as
possible realize you are hurt, which
means it must be before you meet
young Granby today."

"No."

Philip recognized the obstinate look
in the boyish face, but he said calmly:
"If you were to drive your carriage
into a ditch on the way to Crowsham,
it would be easy to postpone your
competition to another day."

"I have never cheated in a race yet,
and I will not begin now. Besides, we
have a wager on it. The race must
stand, it is a matter of honour."

"I am more interested in saving your life, boy!" came the sharp reply. "If you join your friends today, there is no way you can disguise the fact that your right arm is practically useless! How do you intend to manage those bays?"

"With my left hand," muttered Vivyan sullenly.

"And do you think Samuel Granby, or young Thirsby won't notice? I'm beginning to think your wits have gone begging!"

"Damn you, Philip, I won't cry off from this!" cried Vivyan, jumping up. "I've been telling everyone that my team can't be beaten, and offering everyone odds on the fact — if I pull out now I should be the butt of every wit in the county!"

"But at least you would be alive and free! Now do, I beg of you, be sensible. As magistrate Sir Lambert will be bound to investigate Jonas's allegations, however wild they may seem. All I ask is that you arrange a little spill in the lanes. It has happened before, everyone knows it."

"But not to me!" declared Vivyan hotly. "I tell you, brother, I will *not* cry off. I will arrange a tumble after I have proved I can beat the others, and you will have to be satisfied with that!"

Upon these words, he picked up his hat and strode out of the room.

★ ★ ★

"May I come in? I — I did knock but I fear you did not hear me." Miss Hetton hesitated at the library door, her enquiring, rather anxious grey eyes fixed upon the major who was sitting behind his desk. He rose and came towards her.

"Of course. I am sorry, my mind was elsewhere."

"Mr Ashby was asking questions, about Vivyan. Did Stalton tell you?"

"Yes. It seems after that Jonas tried to see Vivyan, but was unsuccessful, and has gone instead to Sir Lambert with his suspicions."

"Oh no! What can be done now?"

"I don't know. Vivyan has just stormed out. I am afraid I handled him rather badly — suggested he should fake an accident before his big race today. His pride won't let him do it, he says it is a matter of honour."

Impulsively she put a hand on his arm.

"Pray don't blame yourself!" she said warmly. "No-one could have tried harder to bring Vivyan about. Perhaps we can still achieve something . . . "

For a full minute he stood still, staring down into the grey-green eyes raised trustingly to his own. Then, with a sudden movement he swept her into his arms, kissing her roughly. At first, her brain immobilized by his action, she returned his kiss, then she pulled away, her eyes filling rapidly with tears.

"Oh please don't," she murmured, her voice catching on a sob. "It cannot be right!"

"I am sorry. It was not my intention to kiss you — at least not yet," he told her, a smile lurking in his eyes.

She did not appear to hear him, but began to pace the room, twisting her hands together as she went.

"I have thought and thought about it," she said, almost to herself. "I *could* not convince myself that it was right for Vivyan and I to marry! He is so young, so energetic! I cannot see him as the sober country squire, at least not for the next ten years! I had made up my mind to tell him so, when there was that silly row with Mr Ashby, and after that I *couldn't* let him down."

"Of course not," he agreed, watching her perambulations with a faint smile.

"And now — all this — how can I possibly cry off at this time? Vivyan needs all the support I can give him — you must understand — " she trailed off as he came towards her and took her agitated fingers in his reassuringly strong hands.

"I *do* understand, my love, but you

know as well as I that you and Vivyan would not suit — it would be a disastrous match, I fear."

"Yes, I too came to that conclusion," she said, ignoring his very improper way of addressing her, "but I thought that perhaps I was being selfish because — "

"Because what, my dearest?" he prompted her gently.

Caroline stared down at her hands, lying passively in his comforting grasp.

"Because my affections are otherwise engaged," she said shyly.

She stole a glance upward and found him regarding her with such a look in his eyes that she quickly lowered her own again, flushing deeply.

"Then my brother must look elsewhere for his wife," returned Philip, taking her into his arms again. This time she did not protest when he kissed her, but when at last he let her go she begged him to consider Vivyan's plight.

"He could well be under arrest by nightfall!" she told him.

"He's a hot-headed young fool," said

the major dispassionately, "but we may still be able to bluff it out. After all, there is no firm evidence against him — Bell has disposed of the horse, the stolen property is now returned, so I am not unhopeful."

He took out his watch.

"It wants but half an hour to dinner. If I know anything of Vivyan he will be dining at the Viking after his race, even if his arm is giving him agony, he'll not admit it, so we cannot look to see him much before midnight. On the other hand Jonas could well bring Sir Lambert back with him at any moment, so I think the best thing we can do is to join Holly for dinner, as though we know nothing of what's afoot."

"Could you not go to Crowsham now and talk to Vivyan?"

"If Sir Lambert does call, he would think it very odd for me to have suddenly decided to dash out. After dinner I'll ride over to the Viking to try if I can get a private word with

Vivyan before he talks to Sir Lambert. We'll find some excuse for his injury, never fear."

★ ★ ★

For Caroline, dinner was like a nightmare from which there was no escape. Time dragged by, Mr Ashby had not returned, and every moment she expected Stalton to announce Sir Lambert. Philip smiled encouragingly at her, but she could not be easy. The food tasted of ashes, and she found her mind was racing on even while she was conversing with Mrs Hollister. As soon as dinner was over, she accompanied Mrs Hollister to the drawing-room, knowing that Philip would order his horse and set out for Crowsham. She was glad that the rain had stopped, and the sun was making a brief appearance. She stood by the drawing-room window looking out over the lawn, where the sunshine sparkled on the wet grass. The brief sunny spell would not last, she thought, for heavy rainclouds were massing on the western horizon, coming in with the tide.

Mrs Hollister was happily engaged with her embroidery, and not wishing for conversation, Caroline made herself comfortable in the window-seat and stared out into the darkening sky, her thoughts wandering. She was brought back to reality by the sight of Bell, Mr Lagallan's groom, running along the drive towards the house. Sensing danger, Caroline murmured an excuse and went out to the hall to meet him. She found him at the front door, asking an astonished Stalton for the major. She moved forward saying with quiet authority: "It's alright, Stalton. I know about this. Come into the library, Bell. Major Lagallan has had to go out, but he has left instructions for you."

Silently the groom followed her into the booklined room, but when the door had closed upon them he said uncomfortably that he wasn't sure he should tell her why he was there.

"Oh pray don't be foolish!" she declared impatiently. "If anything has happened to Mr Lagallan you had best to tell me at once. Major Lagallan left here for the Viking not more than ten minutes past, did you not see him?"

"No, ma'am. I've just come down that road, and passed no-one."

"It is possible he went across country, to avoid being seen," she mused to herself, then aloud: "Where is Mr Lagallan?"

"On his way to the beach, ma'am. He means to race."

"You cannot be serious!" she cried, horrified. "The tide must be on its way in."

The groom nodded, his weather-beaten face very grim.

"Aye, ma'am. High tide's at eight o'clock, and it's a spring tide. That's why I jumped down off the curricle when we got to the end of the lane here and ran to fetch the major. I told the young master I'd not be party to it. With all the rain we've had of late it's going to be almost flood level tonight. It's my opinion Mr Lagallan ain't up to it, not with his arm shot through."

"But I thought the race was to be held this afternoon?"

"So it was, but the rain was so bad the others wouldn't agree to it, so they stayed at the Viking and had an early dinner. Then when the rain stopped after dinner they decided to go ahead."

"And they are gone to the beach now?" asked Caroline, thinking quickly.

"Yes, ma'am."

"Very well. Major Lagallan has ridden to the Viking in search of Vivyan. You had best go after him and tell him what you know. I will go down to the beach to see if I can find Mr Lagallan. Order a horse to be saddled up for me."

Before he could argue the point, she was gone to change her satin slippers for stouter boots, but she decided not to waste time changing into her riding habit, but fastened a cloak over her grey silk, and within ten minutes she was riding out of the gates towards Sandburrows.

* * *

There was a strong wind blowing in off the sea as she reached the crest of the sand dunes and she felt a sudden shock when she saw how high up the beach the waves had already advanced. A few hundred yards from her, between the dunes and the sea, three carriages stood, their teams restlessly moving in their harness, anxious to move away from the thunderous roaring of the waves. Caroline urged her horse downward, and they battled against the wind until they came up to the carriages. Mr Thirsby stared hard at her, giving a polite bow, but obviously bewildered by her presence. Mr Granby too, nodded in her direction, but she ignored them and proceeded to the third carriage where Vivyan was making final adjustments to the harness, his face

261

strained as he attempted to do most of the work with his left hand. At the horses' heads, doing her best to hold them still was a woman, wrapped in a woollen shawl, and as Caroline approached she recognized her as the serving maid from the Viking. The girl subjected Caroline to a long, hard stare, but said nothing.

"Vivyan!" Caroline had to shout to make herself heard, and even then her words were whipped away by the wind. "Vivyan I must talk to you."

He glanced around impatiently as he climbed up into the curricle.

"Hello, Caro. Come to see me win?"

She brought her horse as close as she could to the curricle.

"This is madness!" she cried, "The tide is too high, you will never make it in time."

She saw the bright, feverish glow in his dark eyes, and guessed that he and his companions had been drinking heavily: no sober person would contemplate trying to race the tide.

"I'll not back down!" he shouted back at her. "I suppose Bell told you I was here — damn him! He'll be sorry for going off like that, I'll send him off without a character!"

"Be sensible, Vivyan!" she pleaded, "It's far too dangerous to race now, and the wind is so strong — it wouldn't be a fair test for the horses! Come away from the beach, I need to talk to you — urgently."

"Be content that soon enough I shall be playing the sober husband!" he shouted above the roar of the waves.

Desperately she turned to the other gentlemen, who were already casting doubtful looks at the approaching water.

"Lady's right, Viv. Let's arrange another day," suggested Mr Thirsby, drawing alongside.

"Frightened you'll be beaten, Joseph?"

"Of course he isn't frightened — merely he has more sense!" flashed Caroline angrily.

Vivyan turned towards her, his eyes seemed to burn in his pale face as he threw another taunt at her.

"What about you, Caro — are you afraid to come with me?" he held out his hand. "Come — is it not a wife's duty to be at her husband's side?"

Caroline hesitated. She was getting nowhere with him, perhaps if she were to sit beside him she could make him see sense . . . She kicked her foot free of the stirrup and jumped down from her horse, handing the reins to the now frightened Hannah.

"Take my mare off the beach, and quickly," she commanded her. Without another word she climbed up beside Vivyan.

"I'll show 'em my bays can beat them, even with a passenger to carry!"

She caught the smell of brandy fumes on his breath.

"Vivyan this is madness," she said calmly. "Let us go back to Sandburrows and re-arrange your race. I am sure the others would agree to do so."

"P'raps they would but it's too

late," he replied, waving his opponents alongside.

"To the end?" shouted Vivyan, looking at his friends.

They hesitated, their faces clouded now with doubt about wisdom of their actions. Mr Granby started to say something, but Vivyan ignored it and raised his whip as the signal to start the race. The horses sprang forward in their collars as the three curricles set off at a cracking pace along the beach, the other two gentlemen's grooms barely having time to scramble up on to the backs of their masters' carriages.

Vivyan, the reins held firmly in his left hand, glanced at his passenger.

"Don't worry, my dear, I promise I'll be a very docile husband — call this my final glory!"

"That is what I wished to talk to you about," Caroline raised her voice to make herself heard. "I am not going to marry you."

She thought he had not heard her, for he was urging the bays on, leaving the other carriages behind quite rapidly.

"Vivyan!" her voice held an urgent note as she looked over her shoulder. "The others are turning back — they know it's too late to finish the course."

"They are afraid of being cut off — no judgement, either of 'em," he replied indifferently, not slackening his speed.

"So too am I afraid!"

He turned towards her briefly, his eyes mocking, yet not unkind.

"Poor Caro! You are very wise not to marry me. I'm too wild by half!"

"Please turn back!" she begged him. "You cannot wish to kill us both!"

"Why not?" he laughed, his tone feverish, exultant. "I'm as good as convicted of robbery now, what's left for me? And you surely can't want to be a governess again!"

"What of your horses — they have served you well, I cannot believe you will let them perish!"

The intense, wild look faded from his face: the bays' frantic pace slackened.

Ahead of them, the waves were already clawing at the bank of pebbles that ran the length of the breakwater. It was too late to escape that way. The light was fading now, the sun had retired behind the bank of thick grey cloud looming up over the sea. Vivyan frowned, slowed his team and turned them expertly. Caroline marvelled at the way he handled the frightened animals with only his left hand to control them.

In an instant they were racing back along the beach in a desperate attempt to reach the pass in the sand dunes. The muddy grey foam of the waves was coming even closer, and Caroline knew with a numbing certainty that they would not make it. To their right the spring tide thundered ever closer, licking at the wheels, while to their left the sand dunes formed a high bank, covered by coarse grasses and a wall of impenetrable thorny gorse. Suddenly, on the highest point of the dunes, she spotted a figure, then another. With a cry she pointed and Vivyan, following her outstretched finger, strained his eyes to see who it was.

"It's Philip," he told her.

As he spoke more figures appeared. Vivyan turned his team up towards the dunes, the pace slowing as the wheels dragged in the soft sand. They were still some yards away when the waves overtook them, slowing the pace still further. The frightened horses plunged and screamed as they fought towards the high bank. At last they could go no further with the curricle behind them. The wheels had been sucked into the soft sand and were held firm.

Vivyan jumped down and helped Caroline to alight. They were almost knocked off balance as a wave tumbled into them and on towards the dunes. With Vivyan's left arm supporting her, Caroline struggled through the water. It was not yet above her knees, except when the waves rolled over her, soaking her almost to the top of her head, but the weight of her sodden clothes made every movement difficult. She discarded her cloak to ease the drag of the water. As they reached the dunes they heard someone shout not far above them.

"Catch the rope! The rope, Caroline!"

"My brother stolen the march on me, has he?" Vivyan laughed, a reckless, almost happy note in his voice. "You'll suit, the two of you."

He almost dragged Caroline the last few feet to where they could see the rope swinging before them.

"Blast this useless hand!" he swore as the wet rope slipped from his grasp. Caroline managed to catch it in her wet, numbed fingers and together they managed to secure it around her waist.

"Where are you going?" she cried as Vivyan moved away.

"My horses — " he yelled. "If I let them loose they have a chance."

The waves were crashing around the flimsy curricle and the horses, stamping and snorting, tried to pull free as the water washed around them.

"Vivyan!" Caroline's words were whipped away and Vivyan waded out into the water. The rope tightened around her as the men above began to pull her up and she tried to avoid the scratching, tearing thorns of the gorse bushes. Her clothes hung heavily about her cold limbs, her body was racked with aches, but at last the rope was no longer biting into her waist, there was firm ground beneath her feet, and suddenly she was in Philip's arms.

The moment was brief: Caroline pushed herself free and staggered back to the edge of the bank, peering down into the dark confusion of waves and foam. It was almost impossible to make out any detail now, but she thought she could see the remains of the curricle, overturned now and breaking up, but of the horses or Vivyan there was no sign.

"Vivyan!" she screamed, again and again, until sheer exhaustion forced her to stop and she passed into oblivion.

The first day of the new year was bright and cold. Two figures stood on the top of the grass-covered bank that separated the village of Sandburrows from the beach. A few feet from them the bank dropped sharply away, covered with thick gorse bushes that held the soft sandy soil in place. They were dressed in sombre colours, the lady's grey gown showed briefly as the wind whipped at the opening of her black cloak. The gentleman stood close beside her, one hand protectively under her elbow.

★ ★ ★

Caroline put up her hand to push away a stray curl that the wind carried across her face, and the watery sun gleamed upon the plain wedding band, the only ornament upon her gloveless hands.

"If only he had not gone back for the horses — " she began.

"It was always Vivyan's way, to

attempt the impossible," replied the major gently. He smiled. "As usual to some degree he succeeded, though how those bays managed to get to the pass the Lord only knows."

Impulsively she turned and buried her face in the shoulder capes of his dark driving coat.

"I cannot believe he is gone! It isn't fair that he should die, so young, such a waste — "

Philip put his arms around her.

"You know that I shall not cease to enquire after him, up and down the coast, until there is some proof, one way or the other. But hush, my dear. It would have been infinitely worse for him had he been locked up. One cannot cage a wild animal. As it is we have Sir Lambert's assurance that since there was nothing definite to connect Vivyan with the robberies, and only Ashby's suspicions against him, his character remains unblemished."

He led her gently down to the waiting coach and they returned to

Lagallan House, where Mrs Hollister was looking out for them.

"Come and warm yourself by the fire, Caroline," she said kindly, "You look frozen, poor child. I will fetch you a warm drink, and while I am gone you can read this." She handed Caroline a sealed letter. "One of the village boys brought it over soon after you had gone out. It is addressed to Mrs Philip Lagallan, and I don't doubt it is another note of congratulations upon your marriage. You have received so many I am sure I don't know when there was a more welcome match!"

Philip met his wife's eyes and smiled at her. Caroline broke the seal with her cold fingers and spread the single sheet upon her knees. For a full minute she stared at it, the colour draining from her face.

"Caroline?" Philip's voice was sharp with concern at her rigid pose.

He took the letter from her nerveless hand and scanned it quickly. It was very brief and written in a bold, flowing hand that he recognized at once.

"Congratulations dear sister, you have made the wisest choice."

THE END

Other titles in the Linford Romance Library:

A YOUNG MAN'S FANCY
Nancy Bell

Six people get together for reasons of their own, and the result is one of misunderstanding, suspicion and mounting tension.

THE WISDOM OF LOVE
Janey Blair

Barbie meets Louis and receives flattering proposals, but her reawakened affection for Jonah develops into an overwhelming passion.

MIRAGE IN THE MOONLIGHT
Mandy Brown

En route to an island to be secretary to a multi-millionaire, Heather's stubborn loyalty to her former flatmate plunges her into a grim hazard.

WITH SOMEBODY ELSE
Theresa Charles

Rosamond sets off for Cornwall with Hugo to meet his family, blissfully unaware of the shocks in store for her.

A SUMMER FOR STRANGERS
Claire Hamilton

Because she had lost her job, her flat and she had no money, Tabitha agreed to pose as Adam's future wife although she believed the scheme to be deceitful and cruel.

VILLA OF SINGING WATER
Angela Petron

The disquieting incidents that occurred at the Vatican and the Colosseum did not trouble Jan at first, but then they became increasingly unpleasant and alarming.

DOCTOR NAPIER'S NURSE
Pauline Ash

When cousins Midge and Derry are entered as probationer nurses on the same day but at different hospitals they agree to exchange identities.

A GIRL LIKE JULIE
Louise Ellis

Caroline absolutely adored Hugh Barrington, but then Julie Crane came into their lives. Julie was the kind of girl who attracts men without even trying.

COUNTRY DOCTOR
Paula Lindsay

When Evan Richmond bought a practice in a remote country village he did not realise that a casual encounter would lead to the loss of his heart.

ENCORE
Helga Moray

Craig and Janet realise that their true happiness lies with each other, but it is only under traumatic circumstances that they can be reunited.

NICOLETTE
Ivy Preston

When Grant Alston came back into her life, Nicolette was faced with a dilemma. Should she follow the path of duty or the path of love?

THE GOLDEN PUMA
Margaret Way

Catherine's time was spent looking after her father's Queensland farm. But what life was there without David, who wasn't interested in her?

HOSPITAL BY THE LAKE
Anne Durham

Nurse Marguerite Ingleby was always ready to become personally involved with her patients, to the despair of Brian Field, the Senior Surgical Registrar, who loved her.

VALLEY OF CONFLICT
David Farrell

Isolated in a hostel in the French Alps, Ann Russell sees her fiancé being seduced by a young girl. Then comes the avalanche that imperils their lives.

NURSE'S CHOICE
Peggy Gaddis

A proposal of marriage from the incredibly handsome and wealthy Reagan was enough to upset any girl — and Brooke Martin was no exception.

A DANGEROUS MAN
Anne Goring

Photographer Polly Burton was on safari in Mombasa when she met enigmatic Leon Hammond. But unpredictability was the name of the game where Leon was concerned.

PRECIOUS INHERITANCE
Joan Moules

Karen's new life working for an authoress took her from Sussex to a foreign airstrip and a kidnapping; to a real life adventure as gripping as any in the books she typed.

VISION OF LOVE
Grace Richmond

When Kathy takes over the rundown country kennels she finds Alec Stinton, a local vet, very helpful. But their friendship arouses bitter jealousy and a tragedy seems inevitable.

CRUSADING NURSE
Jane Converse

It was handsome Dr. Corbett who opened Nurse Susan Leighton's eyes and who set her off on a lonely crusade against some powerful enemies and a shattering struggle against the man she loved.

WILD ENCHANTMENT
Christina Green

Rowan's agreeable new boss had a dream of creating a famous perfume using her precious Silverstar, but Rowan's plans were very different.

DESERT ROMANCE
Irene Ord

Sally agrees to take her sister Pam's place as La Chartreuse the dancer, but she finds out there is more to it than dyeing her hair red and looking like her sister.

HEART OF ICE
Marie Sidney

How was January to know that not only would the warmth of the Swiss people thaw out her frozen heart, but that she too would play her part in helping someone to live again?

LUCKY IN LOVE
Margaret Wood

Companion-secretary to wealthy gambler Laura Duxford, who lived in Monaco, seemed to Melanie a fabulous job. Especially as Melanie had already lost her heart to Laura's son, Julian.

NURSE TO PRINCESS JASMINE
Lilian Woodward

Nick's surgeon brother, Tom, performs an operation on an Arabian princess, and she invites Tom, Nick and his fiancé to Omander, where a web of deceit and intrigue closes about them.